F. Anstey

Lyre and lancet

A story in scenes

F. Anstey

Lyre and lancet
A story in scenes

ISBN/EAN: 9783744749299

Printed in Europe, USA, Canada, Australia, Japan

Cover: Foto ©Andreas Hilbeck / pixelio.de

More available books at **www.hansebooks.com**

LYRE AND LANCET

LYRE AND LANCET

A STORY IN SCENES

BY

F. ANSTEY

AUTHOR OF

"VICE VERSÂ," "THE GIANT'S ROBE," "VOCES POPULI," ETC.

LONDON:

SMITH, ELDER & CO., 15, WATERLOO PLACE.

1895.

CONTENTS

PART		PAGE
I.	SHADOWS CAST BEFORE	1
II.	SELECT PASSAGES FROM A COMING POET	11
III.	THE TWO ANDROMEDAS	21
IV.	RUSHING TO CONCLUSIONS	31
V.	CROSS PURPOSES	42
VI.	ROUND PEGS IN SQUARE HOLES	53
VII.	IGNOTUM PRO MIRIFICO	64
VIII.	SURPRISES—AGREEABLE AND OTHERWISE	76
IX.	THE MAUVAIS QUART D'HEURE	87
X.	BORROWED PLUMES	98
XI.	TIME AND THE HOUR	109
XII.	DIGNITY UNDER DIFFICULTIES	119
XIII.	WHAT'S IN A NAME?	130
XIV.	LE VÉTÉRINAIRE MALGRÉ LUI	141
XV.	TRAPPED!	152
XVI.	AN INTELLECTUAL PRIVILEGE	163
XVII.	A BOMB SHELL	174
XVIII.	THE LAST STRAW	184
XIX.	UNEARNED INCREMENT	194
XX.	DIFFERENT PERSONS HAVE DIFFERENT OPINIONS	204
XXI.	THE FEELINGS OF A MOTHER	213
XXII.	A DESCENT FROM THE CLOUDS	224
XXIII.	SHRINKAGE	234
XXIV.	THE HAPPY DISPATCH	244

CHARACTERS

GALFRID UNDERSHELL (*a minor poet*).

JAMES SPURRELL, M.R.C.V.S.

THE COUNTESS OF CANTIRE.

LADY MAISIE MULL (*her daughter*).

SIR RUPERT CULVERIN.

LADY CULVERIN.

LADY RHODA COKAYNE.

MRS. BROOKE-CHATTERIS.

MISS SPELWANE.

THE BISHOP OF BIRCHESTER.

LORD LULLINGTON.

LADY LULLINGTON.

MRS. EARWAKER.

THE HONOURABLE BERTIE PILLINER.

CAPTAIN THICKNESSE.

ARCHIE BEARPARK.

MR. SHORTHORN.

DRYSDALE (*a journalist*).

TANRAKE (*a job-master*).

EMMA PHILLIPSON (**maid to** LADY CANTIRE).

MRS. POMFRET (*housekeeper at Wyvern Court*).

MISS STICKLER (*maid to* LADY CULVERIN).
MISS DOLMAN (**maid to** LADY RHODA COKAYNE).
MLLE. CHIFFON (*maid to* MISS SPELWANE).
M. RIDEVOS (*chef at* Wyvern).
TREDWELL (**butler at** Wyvern).
STEPTOE (*valet to* SIR RUPERT CULVERIN).
THOMAS (*a footman*).
ADAMS (*stud-groom*).
CHECKLEY (*head* **coachman**).
Steward's Room **Boy, etc.**

LYRE AND LANCET

A STORY IN SCENES

———◦◦◦———

PART I

SHADOWS CAST BEFORE

In Sir RUPERT CULVERIN'S *Study at Wyvern Court.*
It is a rainy Saturday morning in February.
Sir RUPERT *is at his writing-table, as* Lady
CULVERIN *enters with a deprecatory air.*

Lady Culverin. So *here* you are, Rupert! Not
very busy, are you? I won't keep you a moment.
(*She goes to a window.*) Such a nuisance it's turning
out wet, with all these people in the house, isn't it?

Sir Rupert. Well, I was thinking that, as there's
nothing doing out of doors, I might get a chance to
knock off some of these confounded accounts, but—
(*resignedly*)—if you think I ought to go and look
after———

B

Lady Culverin. No, no; the men are playing billiards, and the women are in the morning-room —*they*'re all right. I only wanted to ask you about to-night. You know the Lullingtons, and the dear Bishop and Mrs. Rodney, and one or two other people are coming to dinner? Well, who ought to take in Rohesia?

Sir Rupert (in dismay). Rohesia! No idea she was coming down this week!

Lady Culverin. Yes, by the 4.45. With dear Maisie. Surely you knew that?

Sir Rupert. In a sort of way; didn't realize it was so near, that's all.

Lady Culverin. It's some time since we had her last. And she wanted to come. I didn't think you would like me to write and put her off.

Sir Rupert. Put her off? Of course I shouldn't, Albinia. If my only sister isn't welcome at Wyvern at any time—I say at *any* time—where the deuce *is* she welcome?

Lady Culverin. I don't know, dear Rupert. But —but about the table?

Sir Rupert. So long as you don't put her near me—that's all *I* care about.

Lady Culverin. I mean—ought I to send her in with Lord Lullington, or the Bishop?

Sir Rupert. Why not let 'em toss up ?   Loser gets her, of course.

Lady Culverin. Rupert !   As if I could suggest such a thing to the Bishop ! I suppose she'd better go in with Lord Lullington—he's Lord Lieutenant— and then it won't matter if she *does* advocate Disestablishment.   Oh, but I forgot; she thinks the House of Lords ought to be abolished *too !*

Sir Rupert. Whoever takes Rohesia in is likely to have a time of it.   Talked poor Cantire into his tomb a good ten years before he was due there. Always lecturing, and domineering, and laying down the law, as long as *I* can remember her.   Can't stand Rohesia—never could !

Lady Culverin. I don't think you ought to say so, really, Rupert.   And I'm sure *I* get on very well with her—generally.

Sir Rupert. Because you knock under to her.

Lady Culverin. I'm sure I don't, Rupert—at least, no more than everybody else.   Dear Rohesia is so strong-minded and advanced and all that, she takes such an interest in all the new movements and things, that she can't understand contradiction; she is so democratic in her ideas, don't you know.

Sir Rupert. Didn't prevent her marrying Cantire.

And a democratic Countess—it's downright unnatural!

Lady Culverin. She believes it's her duty to set
an example and meet the People half-way. That
reminds me—did I tell you Mr. Clarion Blair is
coming down this evening, too?—only till Monday,
Rupert.

Sir Rupert. Clarion Blair! never heard of him.

Lady Culverin. I suppose I forgot. Clarion Blair
isn't his *real* name, though; it's only a—an alias.

Sir Rupert. Don't see what any fellow wants with
an alias. What *is* his real name?

Lady Culverin. Well, I know it was *something*
ending in "ell," but I mislaid his letter. Still,
Clarion Blair is the name he writes under; he's a
poet, Rupert, and quite celebrated, so I'm told.

Sir Rupert (uneasily). A poet! What on earth
possessed you to ask a literary fellow down *here?*
Poetry isn't much in our way; and a poet *will* be,
confoundedly!

Lady Culverin. I really couldn't help it, Rupert.
Rohesia insisted on my having him to meet her.
She likes meeting clever and interesting people.
And this Mr. Blair, it seems, has just written a
volume of verses which are finer than anything that's
been done since—well, for *ages!*

"WHAT ON EARTH POSSESSED YOU TO ASK A LITERARY FELLOW DOWN HERE?"

Sir Rupert. What sort of verses?

Lady Culverin. Well, they're charmingly bound. I've got the book in the house, somewhere. Rohesia told me to send for it; but I haven't had time to read it yet.

Sir Rupert. Shouldn't be surprised if Rohesia hadn't, either.

Lady Culverin. At all events, she's heard it talked about. The young man's verses have made quite a sensation; they're so dreadfully clever and revolutionary, and morbid and pessimistic, and all that, so she made me promise to ask him down here to meet her!

Sir Rupert. Devilish thoughtful of her.

Lady Culverin. Wasn't it? She thought it might be a valuable experience for him; he's sprung, I believe, from *quite* the middle-class.

Sir Rupert. Don't see myself why he should be sprung on *us*. Why can't Rohesia ask him to one of her own places?

Lady Culverin. I dare say she will, if he turns out to be quite presentable. And, of course, he *may*, Rupert, for anything we can tell.

Sir Rupert. Then you've never seen him yourself! How did you manage to ask him here, then?

Lady Culverin. Oh, I wrote to him through his

publishers. Rohesia says that's the usual way with literary persons one doesn't happen to have met. And he wrote to say he would come.

Sir Rupert. So we're to have a morbid revolutionary poet staying in the house, are we? He'll come down to dinner in a flannel shirt and no tie—or else a *red* one—if he don't bring down a beastly bomb and try to blow us all up! You'll find you've made a mistake, Albinia, depend upon it.

Lady Culverin. Dear Rupert, aren't you just a little bit *narrow?* You forget that nowadays the very best houses are proud to entertain Genius—no matter *what* their opinions and appearance may be. And besides, we don't know what changes may be coming. Surely it is wise and prudent to conciliate the clever young men who might inflame the masses against us. Rohesia thinks so; she says it may be our only chance of stemming the rising tide of Revolution, Rupert!

Sir Rupert. Oh, if Rohesia thinks a revolution can be stemmed by asking a few poets down from Saturday to Monday, she might do *her* share of the stemming at all events.

Lady Culverin. But you will be *nice* to him, Rupert, won't you?

Sir Rupert. I don't know that I'm in the habit

of being uncivil to any guest of yours in this house, my dear, but I'll be hanged if I *grovel* to him, you know; the tide ain't as high as all that. But it's an infernal nuisance, 'pon my word it is; you must look after him yourself. *I* can't. I don't know what to talk to geniuses about; I've forgotten all the poetry I ever learnt. And if he comes out with any of his Red Republican theories in *my* hearing, why——

Lady Culverin. Oh, but he *won't*, dear. I'm certain he'll be quite mild and inoffensive. Look at Shakespeare—the bust, I mean—and *he* began as a poacher!

Sir Rupert. Ah, and this chap would put down the Game Laws if he could, I dare say; do away with everything that makes the country worth living in. Why, if he had his way, Albinia, there wouldn't be——

Lady Culverin. I know, dear, I know. And you must make him see all that from *your* point. Look, the weather really seems to be clearing a little. We might all of us get out for a drive or something after lunch. I would ride, if Deerfoot's all right again; he's the only horse I ever feel *really* safe upon, now.

Sir Rupert. Sorry, my dear, but you'll have to drive then. Adams tells me the horse is as lame as ever this morning, and he don't know what to make of it. He suggested having Horsfall over, but I've no faith in the local vets myself, so I wired to town for old Spavin. He's seen Deerfoot before, and we could put him up for a night or two. (*To* TREDWELL, *the butler, who enters with a telegram.*) Eh, for me? just wait, will you, in case there's an answer. (*As he opens it.*) Ah, this *is* from Spavin—h'm, nuisance! "Regret unable to leave at present, bronchitis, junior partner could attend immediately if required.— Spavin." Never knew he *had* a partner.

Tredwell. I did hear, Sir Rupert, as Mr. Spavin was looking out for one quite recent, being hasthmatical, m'lady, and so I suppose this is him as the telegram alludes to.

Sir Rupert. Very likely. Well, he's sure to be a competent man. We'd better have him, eh, Albinia?

Lady Culverin. Oh yes, and he must stay till Deerfoot's better. I'll speak to Pomfret about having a room ready in the East Wing for him. Tell him to come by the 4.45, Rupert. We shall be sending the omnibus in to meet that.

Sir Rupert. All right, I've told him. (*Giving the form to* TREDWELL.) See that that's sent off at once, please. (*After* TREDWELL *has left.*) By the way,

Albinia, Rohesia may kick up a row if she has to come up in the omnibus with a vet, eh?

Lady Culverin. Goodness, so she might! but he needn't go *inside*. Still, if it goes on raining like this—I'll tell Thomas to order a fly for him at the station, and then there *can't* be any bother about it.

PART II

SELECT PASSAGES FROM A COMING POET

In the Morning Room at Wyvern. Lady RHODA COKAYNE, Mrs. BROOKE-CHATTERIS, *and* Miss VIVIEN SPELWANE *are comfortably established near the fireplace. The* Hon. BERTIE PILLINER, Captain THICKNESSE, *and* ARCHIE BEARPARK, *have just drifted in.*

Miss Spelwane. Why, you *don't* mean to say you've torn yourselves away from your beloved billiards already ? *Quite* wonderful !

Bertie Pilliner. It's too *horrid* of you to leave us to play all by ourselves ! We've all got so cross and fractious we've come in here to be petted !

> [*He arranges himself at her feet, so as to exhibit a very neat pair of silk socks and pumps.*

Captain Thicknesse (to himself). Do hate to see a fellow come down in the mornin' with evenin' shoes on !

Archie Bearpark (to BERTIE PILLINER). You speak for yourself, PILLINER. *I* didn't come to be petted. Came to see if Lady Rhoda wouldn't come and toboggan down the big staircase on a tea-tray. *Do!* It's clinkin' sport!

Captain Thicknesse (to himself). If there's one thing I *can't* stand, it's a rowdy bullyraggin' ass like Archie!

Lady Rhoda Cokayne. Ta muchly, dear boy, but you don't catch me travellin' downstairs on a tea-tray *twice*—it's just a bit *too* clinkin', don't you know!

Archie Bearpark (disappointed). Why, there's a mat at the bottom of the stairs! Well, if you won't, let's get up a cushion fight, then. Bertie and I will choose sides. Pilliner, I'll toss you for first pick up —come out of that, do.

Bertie Pilliner (lazily). Thanks, I'm much too comfy where I am. And I don't see any point in romping and rumpling one's hair just before lunch.

Archie Bearpark. Well, you *are* slack. And there's a good hour still before lunch. Thicknesse, *you* suggest something, there's a dear old chap.

Captain Thicknesse (after a mental effort). Suppose we all go and have another look round at the gees — eh, what?

Bertie Pilliner. I beg to oppose.   Do let's show *some* respect for the privacy of the British hunter. Why should I go and smack them on their fat backs, and feel every one of their horrid legs twice in one morning?   I shouldn't like a horse coming into my bedroom at all hours to smack *me* on the back.   I should *hate* it!

Mrs. Brooke-Chatteris. I love them—dear things! But still, it's so wet, and it would mean going up and changing our shoes too—perhaps Lady Rhoda——

[Lady RHODA *flatly declines to stir before lunch.*

Captain Thicknesse (resentfully). Only thought it was better than loafin' about, that's all.   (*To himself.*) I do bar a woman who's afraid of a little mud.   (*He saunters up to* Miss SPELWANE *and absently pulls the ear of a Japanese spaniel on her knee.*)   Poo' little fellow, then!

Miss Spelwane. Poor little fellow?   On *my* lap!

Captain Thicknesse. Oh, it—ah—didn't occur to me that he was on *your* lap.   He don't seem to mind *that.*

Miss Spelwane. No?   *How* forbearing of him! Would you mind not standing quite so much in my light?   I can't see my work.

Captain Thicknesse (to himself, retreating). That girl's always fishin' for compliments.   I didn't rise *that* time, though. It's precious slow here. I've a good mind to say I must get back to Aldershot this afternoon.

> [*He wanders aimlessly about the room ;* ARCHIE
> BEARPARK *looks out of window with un-*
> *disguised boredom.*

Lady Rhoda. I say, if none of you are goin' to be more amusin' than this, you may as well go back to your billiards again.

Bertie Pilliner. Dear Lady Rhoda, how cruel of you! You'll have to let *me* stay. I'll be *so* good. Look here, I'll read aloud to you. I *can*—quite prettily. What shall it be? You don't care? No more do I. I'll take the first that comes. (*He reaches for the nearest volume on a table close by.*) How *too* delightful! Poetry—which I know you *all* adore. [*He turns over the leaves.*

Lady Rhoda. If you ask *me*, I simply loathe it.

Bertie Pilliner. Ah, but then you never heard *me* read it, you know. Now, here is a choice little bit, stuck right up in a corner, as if it had been mis-behaving itself. "Disenchantment" it's called.

> [*He reads.*

" My Love has sicklied unto Loath,
   And foul seems all that fair I fancied —
The lily's sheen a leprous growth,
   The very buttercups are rancid!"

Archie Bearpark. Jove! The Johnny who wrote that must have been feelin' chippy!

Bertie Pilliner. He gets cheaper than that in the next poem. This is his idea of "Abasement."

[*He reads.*

> "With matted head a-dabble in the dust,
>   And eyes tear-sealèd in a saline crust,
>   I lie all loathly in my rags and rust—
> Yet learn that strange delight may lurk in self-disgust."

Now, do you know, I rather like that—it's so deliciously decadent!

Lady Rhoda. I should call it utter rot, myself.

Bertie Pilliner (*blandly*). Forgive me, Lady Rhoda. "Utterly rotten," if you like, but *not* "utter rot." There's a difference, really. Now, I'll read you a quaint little production which has dropped down to the bottom of the page, in low spirits, I suppose. "Stanza written in Depression near Dulwich."

[*He reads.*

> "The lark soars up in the air;
>   The toad sits tight in his hole;
>   And I would I were certain which of the pair
> Were the truer type of my soul!"

Archie Bearpark. I should be inclined to back the toad, myself.

Miss Spelwane. If you must read, do choose

"NOW I'LL READ YOU A REGULAR ROUSER CALLED 'A TRUMPET BLAST.'"

something a little less dismal.   Aren't there any love songs?

Bertie Pilliner. I'll look.   Yes, any amount— here's one.   (*He reads.*)   "To My Lady."

> " Twine, lanken fingers lily-lithe,
>   Gleam, slanted eyes all beryl-green,
> Pout, blood-red lips that burst awrithe,
>   Then—kiss me, Lady Grisoline!"

Miss Spelwane (*interested*).   So *that's* his type. Does he mention whether she *did* kiss him?

Bertie Pilliner. Probably.   Poets are always privileged to kiss and tell.   I'll see . . . h'm, ha, yes; he *does* mention it. . . . I think I'll read something else.   Here's a classical specimen.   [*He reads.*

> " Uprears the monster now his slobberous head,
>   Its filamentous chaps her ankles brushing;
> Her twice-five roseal toes are cramped in dread,
>   Each maidly instep mauven-pink is flushing."

And so on, don't you know. . . . Now I'll read you a regular rouser called " A Trumpet Blast."   Sit tight, everybody!   [*He reads.*

> " Pale Patricians, sunk in self-indulgence, (One for *you*, dear
>   Archie!)
>   Blink your bleared eyes.   (Blink, pretty creatures, blink!)
>   Behold the Sun-
>   -Burst proclaim, in purpurate effulgence,
>   Demos dawning, and the Darkness—done!"

> [*General hilarity, amidst which* Lady CULVERIN
>   *enters.*

C

Lady Culverin. So *glad* you all contrive to keep your spirits up, in spite of this dismal weather. What is it that's amusing you all so much, eh, dear Vivien?

Miss Spelwane. Bertie Pilliner has been reading aloud to us, dear Lady Culverin—*the* most ridiculous poetry—made us all simply shriek. What's the name of it? (*Taking the volume out of* BERTIE'S *hand.*) Oh, *Andromeda, and other Poems.* By Clarion Blair.

Lady Culverin (*coldly*). Bertie Pilliner can turn everything into ridicule, we all know; but probably you are not aware that these particular poems are considered quite wonderful by all competent judges. Indeed, my sister-in-law——

All (*in consternation*). Lady Cantire! Is *she* the author? Oh, of course, if we'd had any idea——

Lady Culverin. I've no reason to believe that Lady Cantire ever composed *any* poetry. I was only going to say that she was most interested in the author, and as she and my niece Maisie are coming to us this evening——

Miss Spelwane. Dear Lady Culverin, the verses are quite, *quite* beautiful; it was only the way they were read.

Lady Culverin. I am glad to hear you say so, my

dear, because I'm also expecting the pleasure of seeing the author here, and you will probably be his neighbour to-night. I hope, Bertie, that you will remember that this young man is a very distinguished genius; there is no wit that *I* can discover in making fun of what one doesn't happen to understand.   [*She passes on.*

Bertie (*plaintively, after* Lady CULVERIN *has left the room*). May I trouble somebody to scrape me up? I'm pulverised! But really, you know, a real live poet at Wyvern! I say, Miss Spelwane, how will you like to have him dabbling his matted head next to you at dinner, eh?

Miss Spelwane. Perhaps I shall find a matted head more entertaining than a smooth one. And, if you've quite done with that volume, *I* should like to have a look at it.   [*She retires, with it to her room.*

Archie (*to himself*). I'm not half sorry this Poet-johnny's comin'; I never caught a Bard in a booby-trap *yet*.

Captain Thicknesse (*to himself*). She's coming—this very evenin'! And I was nearly sayin' I must get back to Aldershot!

Lady Rhoda. So Lady Cantire's comin'; we shall all have to be on our hind legs now! But Maisie's a dear thing. Do you know her, Captain Thicknesse?

Captain Thicknesse. I—I used to meet Lady Maisie Mull pretty often at one time; don't know if she'll remember it, though.

Lady Rhoda. She'll love meetin' this writin' man—she's so fearfully romantic. I heard her say once that she'd give anythin' to be idealized by a great poet—sort of—what's their names—Petrarch and Beatrice business, don't you know. It will be rather amusin' to see whether it comes off—won't it?

Captain Thicknesse (choking). I—ah—no affair of mine, really. (*To himself.*) I'm not intellectual enough for her, I know that. Suppose I shall have to stand by and look on at the Petrarchin'. Well, there's always Aldershot!

> [*The luncheon gong sounds, to the general relief and satisfaction*

PART III

THE TWO ANDROMEDAS

Opposite a Railway Bookstall at a London Terminus.
TIME—*Saturday,* 4.25 P.M.

Drysdale (*to his friend,* GALFRID UNDERSHELL, *whom he is " seeing off "*). Twenty minutes to spare; time enough to lay in any quantity of light literature.

Undershell (*in a head voice*). I fear the merely ephemeral does not appeal to me. But I should like to make a little experiment. (*To the* Bookstall Clerk.) A—do you happen to have a copy left of Clarion Blair's *Andromeda* ?

Clerk. Not in stock, sir. Never 'eard of the book, but dare say I could get it for you. Here's a Detective Story we're sellin' like 'ot cakes—*The Man with the Missing Toe*—very cleverly written story, sir.

Undershell. I merely wished to know—that was all. (*Turning with resigned disgust to* DRYSDALE.)

"HERE'S A DETECTIVE STORY WE'RE SELLING LIKE 'OT CAKES."

Just think of it, my dear fellow. At a bookstall like this one feels the pulse, as it were, of Contemporary Culture; and here my *Andromeda*, which no less an authority than the *Daily Chronicle* hailed as the uprising of a new and splendid era in English Song-making, a Poetic Renascence, my poor *Andromeda*, is trampled underfoot by—(*choking*)—Men with Missing Toes! What a satire on our so-called Progress!

Drysdale. That a purblind public should prefer a Shilling Shocker for railway reading when for a modest half-guinea they might obtain a numbered volume of Coming Poetry on hand-made paper! It *does* seem incredible,—but they do. Well, if they can't read *Andromeda* on the journey, they can at least peruse a stinger on it in this week's *Saturday.* Seen it?

Undershell. No. I don't vex my soul by reading criticisms on my work. I am no Keats. They may howl—but they will not kill *me.* By the way, the *Speaker* had a most enthusiastic notice last week.

Drysdale. So you saw *that* then? But you're right not to mind the others. When a fellow's contrived to hang on to the Chariot of Fame, he can't wonder if a few rude and envious beggars call out "Whip behind!" eh? You don't want to get

in yet ?   Suppose we take a turn up to the end of
the platform.   [*They do.*

JAMES SPURRELL, **M.R.C.V.S.**, *enters with his friend,*
     THOMAS TANRAKE, *of* HURDELL AND TANRAKE,
     Job and Riding Masters, **Mayfair**.

Spurrell. **Yes,** it's lucky for me old Spavin being
laid up like this—gives me a regular little outing,
do you see ? going down to a swell place like this
Wyvern Court, and being put up there for a day or
two !   I shouldn't wonder if they do you very well
in the housekeeper's room.   (*To* Clerk.)   Give me a
Pink Un and last week's *Dog Fancier's Guide.*

Clerk. **We've** returned the unsold copies, sir.
Could give you *this* week's; or there's *The Rabbit
and Poultry Breeder's Journal.*

Spurrell. **Oh,** rabbits be blowed !   (*To* TANRAKE.)
I wanted you to see that notice they put in of
Andromeda and me, with my photo and all; it said
she was the best bull-bitch they'd seen for many a
day, and fully deserved her first prize

Tanrake. **She's** a rare good bitch, and no mistake.
But what made you call her such an outlandish name ?

Spurrell. **Well,** I *was* going to call her Sal ; but
a chap at the College thought the other would
look more stylish if I ever meant to 'exhibit her.

Andromeda was one of them Roman goddesses, you know.

Tanrake. Oh, I knew *that* right enough. Come and have a drink before you start—just for luck—not that you want *that.*

Spurrell. I'm lucky enough in most things, Tom; in everything except love. I told you about that girl, you know—Emma—and my being as good as engaged to her, and then, all of a sudden, she went off abroad, and I've never seen or had a line from her since. Can't call *that* luck, you know. Well, I won't say no to a glass of something.

[*They disappear into the refreshment room.*

The Countess of CANTIRE *enters with her daughter,* Lady MAISIE MULL.

Lady Cantire (to Footman). Get a compartment for us, and two foot-warmers, and a second-class as near ours as you can for Phillipson ; then come back here. Stay, I'd better give you Phillipson's ticket. (*The* Footman *disappears in the crowd.*) Now we must get something to read on the journey. (*To* Clerk.) I want a book of some sort—no rubbish, mind ; something serious and improving, and *not* a work of fiction.

Clerk. Exactly so, ma'am. Let me see. Ah,

here's *Alone with the 'Airy Ainoo.* How would you like *that?*

Lady Cantire (with decision). I should not like it at all.

Clerk. I quite understand. Well, I can give you *Three 'Undred Ways of Dressing the Cold Mutton*— useful little book for a family, redooced to one and ninepence.

Lady Cantire. Thank you. I think I will wait till I am reduced to one and ninepence.

Clerk. Precisely. What do you say to *Seven 'Undred Side-splitters for Sixpence?* 'Ighly yumerous, I assure you.

Lady Cantire. Are these times to split our sides, with so many serious social problems pressing for solution? You are presumably not without intelligence; do you never reflect upon the responsibility you incur in assisting to circulate trivial and frivolous trash of this sort?

Clerk (dubiously). Well, I can't say as I do, particular, ma'am. I'm paid to sell the books—I don't *select* 'em.

Lady Cantire. That is *no* excuse for you—you ought to exercise some discrimination on your own account, instead of pressing people to buy what can do them no possible good. You can give me a *Society Snippets.*

Lady Maisie. Mamma! A penny paper that says such rude things about the Royal Family!

Lady Cantire. It's always instructive to know what these creatures are saying about one, my dear, and it's astonishing how they manage to find out the things they do. Ah, here's Gravener coming back. He's got us a carriage, and we'd better get in.

> [*She and her daughter enter a first-class compartment;* UNDERSHELL *and* DRYSDALE *return.*

Drysdale (*to* UNDERSHELL). Well, I don't see now where the insolence comes in. These people have invited you to stay with them——

Undershell. But why? Not because they appreciate my work—which they probably only half understand—but out of mere idle curiosity to see what manner of strange beast a Poet may be! And *I* don't know this Lady Culverin—never met her in my life! What the deuce does she mean by sending me an invitation? Why should these smart women suppose that they are entitled to send for a Man of Genius, as if he was their *lackey?* Answer me that!

Drysdale. Perhaps the delusion is encouraged by the fact that Genius occasionally condescends to answer the bell.

Undershell (*reddening*). Do you imagine I am going down to this place simply to please *them?*

Drysdale. I should think it a doubtful kindness, in your present frame of mind; and, as you are hardly going to please yourself, wouldn't it be more dignified, on the whole, not to go at all?

Undershell. You never *did* understand me! Sometimes I think I was born to be misunderstood! But you might do me the justice to believe that I am not going from merely snobbish motives. May I not feel that such a recognition as this is a tribute less to my poor self than to Literature, and that, as such, I have scarcely the *right* to decline it?

Drysdale. Ah, if you put it in that way, I am silenced, of course.

Undershell. Or what if I am going to show these Patricians that—Poet of the People as I am—they can neither patronise nor cajole me?

Drysdale. Exactly, old chap—what if you *are?*

Undershell. I don't say that I may not have another reason—a—a rather romantic one—but you would only sneer if I told you! I know you think me a poor creature whose head has been turned by an undeserved success.

Drysdale. You're not going to try to pick a quarrel with an old chum, are you? Come, you know well enough I don't think anything of the sort. I've always said you had the right stuff in you, and would show it some day; there are even signs of it in *Andromeda* here and there; but you'll do better things than that, if you'll only let some of the wind out of your head. I take an interest in you, old fellow, and that's just why it riles me to see you taking yourself so devilish seriously on the strength of a little volume of verse which—between you and me—has been " boomed " for all it's worth, and considerably more. You've only got your immortality on a short repairing lease at present, old boy !

Undershell (with bitterness). I am fortunate in possessing such a candid friend. But I mustn't keep you here any longer.

Drysdale. Very well. I suppose you're going first ? Consider the feelings of the Culverin footman at the other end !

Undershell (as he fingers a first-class ticket in his pocket). You have a very low view of human nature ! (*Here he becomes aware of a remarkably pretty face at a second-class window close by*). As it *happens*, I am travelling second. [*He gets in.*

Drysdale (at the window). Well, good-bye, old chap. Good luck to you at Wyvern, and remember—wear your livery with as good a grace as possible.

Undershell. I do not intend to wear any livery whatever.

> [*The owner of the pretty face regards* UNDER-
> SHELL *with interest.*

Spurrell (*coming out of the refreshment room*). What, second—with all my exes. paid ? Not *likely !* I'm going to travel in style this journey. No— not a smoker ; don't want to create a bad impression, you know. This will do for me.

> [*He gets into a compartment occupied by* Lady
> CANTIRE *and her daughter.*

Tanrake (*at the window*). There—you're off now. Pleasant journey to you, old man. Hope you'll enjoy yourself at this Wyvern Court you're going to—and, I say, don't forget to send me that notice of Andromeda when you get back !

> [*The* Countess *and* Lady MAISIE *start slightly ;*
> *the train moves out of the station.*

PART IV

In a First-class Compartment.

Spurrell (*to himself*).   Formidable old party opposite me in the furs! Nice-looking girl over in the corner; not a patch on my Emma, though! Wonder why I catch 'em sampling me over their papers whenever I look up! Can't be anything wrong with my turn out.   Why, of course, they heard Tom talk about my going down to Wyvern Court; think I'm a visitor there and no end of a duke! Well, what snobs some people are, to be sure!

Lady Cantire (*to herself*). So this is the young poet I made Albinia ask to meet me. I can't be mistaken, I distinctly heard his friend mention *Andromeda.*   H'm, well, it's a comfort to find he's *clean!*   Have I read his poetry or not? I know I *had* the book, because I distinctly remember telling Maisie she wasn't to read it—but—well, that's of no

consequence. He looks clever and quite respectable
—not in the least picturesque—which is fortunate.
I was beginning to doubt whether it was quite
prudent to bring Maisie; but I needn't have worried
myself.

Lady Maisie (to herself). Here, actually in the
same carriage! Does he guess who *I* am? Somehow—— Well, he certainly *is* different from what
I expected. I thought he would show more signs
of having thought and suffered; for he *must* have
suffered to write as he does. If mamma knew I had
read his poems; that I had actually written to beg
him not to refuse Aunt Albinia's invitation! He
never wrote back. Of course I didn't put any
address; but still, he could have found out from the
Red Book if he'd cared. I'm rather glad now he
didn't care.

Spurrell (to himself). Old girl seems as if she
meant to be sociable; better give her an opening.
(*Aloud.*) Hem! would you like the window down
an inch or two?

Lady Cantire. Not on *my* account, thank you.

Spurrell (to himself). Broke the ice, anyway.
(*Aloud.*) Oh, *I* don't want it down, but some people
have such a mania for fresh air.

Lady Cantire (with a dignified little shiver). Have

they? With a temperature as glacial as it is in here! They must be maniacs indeed!

Spurrell. Well, it *is* chilly; been raw all day. (*To himself.*) She don't answer. I *haven't* broken the ice. [*He produces a memorandum book.*

Lady Maisie (*to herself*). He hasn't said anything *very* original yet. So *nice* of him not to pose! Oh, he's got a note-book; he's going to compose a poem. How interesting!

Spurrell (*to himself*). Yes, I'm all right if Heliograph wins the Lincolnshire Handicap; lucky to get on at the price I did. Wonder what's the latest about the City and Suburban? Let's see whether the Pink Un has anything about it.

[*He refers to the Sporting Times.*

Lady Maisie (*to herself*). The inspiration's stopped —*what* a pity! How odd of him to read the *Globe!* I thought he was a Democrat!

Lady Cantire. Maisie, there's quite a clever little notice in *Society Snippets* about the dance at Skympings last week. I'm sure I wonder how they pick up these things; it quite bears out what I was told; says the supper arrangements were "simply disgraceful; not nearly enough champagne; and what there was, undrinkable!" So *like* poor dear Lady Chesepare; never *does* do

D

things like anybody else. I'm sure *I've* given her hints enough!

Spurrell (*to himself, with a suppressed grin*). Wants to let me see *she* knows some swells. Now *ain't* that paltry?

Lady Cantire (*tendering the paper*). Would you like to see it, Maisie? Just this bit here; where my finger is.

Lady Maisie (*to herself, flushing*). I saw him smile. What *must* he think of us, with his splendid scorn for rank? (*Aloud.*) No, thank you, mamma: such a wretched light to read by!

Spurrell (*to himself*). Chance for *me* to cut in! (*Aloud.*) Beastly light, isn't it? 'Pon my word, the company ought to provide us with a dog and string apiece when we get out!

Lady Cantire (*bringing a pair of long-handled glasses to bear upon him*). I happen to hold shares in this line. May I ask *why* you consider a provision of dogs and string at all the stations a necessary or desirable expenditure?

Spurrell. Oh—er—well, you know, I only meant, bring on *blindness* and that. Harmless attempt at a joke, that's all.

Lady Cantire. I see. I scarcely expected that *you* would condescend to such weakness. I—ah—think

you are going down to stay at Wyvern for a few
days, are you not?

Spurrell (*to himself*). I was right. What Tom
said *did* fetch the old girl; no harm in humouring
her a bit. (*Aloud.*) Yes—oh yes, they—aw—
wanted me to run down when I could.

Lady Cantire. I heard they were expecting you. You
will find Wyvern a pleasant house—for a short visit.

Spurrell (*to himself*). *She* heard! Oh, she wants
to kid me she knows the Culverins. Rats! (*Aloud.*)
Shall I, though? I dare say.

Lady Cantire. Lady Culverin is **a** very sweet
woman; a little limited, perhaps, not intellectual, or
quite what one would call the *grande dame;* but
perhaps *that* could scarcely be expected.

Spurrell (*vaguely*). Oh, of course not—no. (*To
himself.*) If she bluffs, so can I! (*Aloud.*) It's
funny your turning out to be an acquaintance of
Lady C.'s, though.

Lady Cantire. You think so? But I should
hardly call myself an *acquaintance.*

Spurrell (*to himself*). Old cat's trying to back out
of it now; she *shan't,* though! (*Aloud.*) Oh, then
I suppose you know Sir Rupert best?

Lady Cantire. Yes, I certainly know Sir Rupert
better.

Spurrell (*to himself*). Oh, you do, do you? We'll see. (*Aloud.*) Nice cheery old chap, Sir Rupert, isn't he? I must tell him I travelled down in the same carriage with a particular friend of his. (*To himself.*) That'll make her sit up!

Lady Cantire. Oh, then you and my brother Rupert have met already?

Spurrell (*aghast*). Your brother! Sir Rupert Culverin your——! Excuse me—if I'd only known, I —I do assure you I never should have dreamt of saying——!

Lady Cantire (*graciously*). You've said nothing whatever to distress yourself about. You couldn't possibly be expected to know who I was. Perhaps I had better tell you at once that I am Lady Cantire, and this is my daughter, Lady Maisie Mull. (SPUR-RELL *returns* Lady MAISIE's *little bow in the deepest confusion.*) We are going down to Wyvern too, so I hope we shall very soon become better acquainted.

Spurrell (*to himself, overwhelmed*). The deuce we shall! I *have* got myself into a hole this time; I wish I could see my way well out of it! Why on earth couldn't I hold my confounded tongue? I *shall* look an ass when I tell 'em.

[*He sits staring at them in silent embarrassment.*

In a Second-class Compartment.

Undershell (*to himself*). Singularly attractive face
this girl has; so piquant and so refined! I can't
help fancying she is studying me under her eye-
lashes. She has remarkably bright eyes. Can she
be interested in me? Does she expect me to talk to
her? There are only she and I—but no, just now I
would rather be alone with my thoughts. This
Maisie Mull whom I shall meet so soon; what is
she like, I wonder? I presume she is unmarried.
If I may judge from her artless little letter, she is
young and enthusiastic, and she is a passionate
admirer of my verse; she is longing to meet me.
I suppose some men's vanity would be flattered by
a tribute like that. I think I must have none; for
it leaves me strangely cold. I did not even reply;
it struck me that it would be difficult to do so with
any dignity, and she didn't tell me where to write
to. . . . After all, how do I know that this will
not end—like everything else—in disillusion? Will
not such crude girlish adoration pall upon me in
time? If she were exceptionally lovely; or say,
even as charming as this fair fellow-passenger of
mine—why then, to be sure—but no, something
warns me that that is not to be. I shall find her

plain, sandy, freckled; she will render me ridiculous by her undiscriminating gush. . . . Yes, I feel my heart sink more and more at the prospect of this visit. Ah me! [*He sighs heavily.*

His Fellow Passenger (*to herself*). It's too silly to be sitting here like a pair of images, considering that—— (*Aloud.*) I hope you aren't feeling unwell?

Undershell. Thank you, no, not unwell. I was merely thinking.

His Fellow Passenger. You don't seem very cheerful over it, I must say. I've no wish to be inquisitive, but perhaps you're feeling a little low-spirited about the place you're going to?

Undershell. I—I must confess I am rather dreading the prospect. How wonderful that you should have guessed it!

His Fellow Passenger. Oh, I've been through it myself. I'm just the same when *I* go down to a new place; feel a sort of sinking, you know, as if the people were sure to be disagreeable, and I should never get on with them.

Undershell. Exactly my own sensations! If I could only be sure of finding *one* kindred spirit, one soul who would help and understand me. But I daren't let myself hope even for that!

His Fellow Passenger. Well, I wouldn't judge beforehand. The chances are there'll be *somebody* you can take to.

Undershell (*to himself*). What sympathy! What bright, cheerful common sense! (*Aloud.*) Do you know, you encourage me more than you can possibly imagine!

His Fellow Passenger (*retreating*). Oh, if you are going to take my remarks like *that*, I shall be afraid to go on talking to you!

Undershell (*with pathos*). Don't—*don't* be afraid to talk to me! If you only knew the comfort you give! I have found life very sad, very solitary. And true sympathy is so rare, so refreshing. I—I fear such an appeal from a stranger may seem a little startling; it is true that hitherto we have only exchanged a very few sentences; and yet already I feel that we have something—much—in common. You can't be so cruel as to let all intimacy cease here—it is quite tantalising enough that it must end so soon. A very few more minutes, and this brief episode will be only a memory; I shall have left the little green oasis far behind me, and be facing the dreary desert once more—alone!

His Fellow Passenger (*laughing*). Well, of all the uncomplimentary things! As it happens, though, "the little green oasis"—as you're kind enough to call me—*won't* be left behind; not if it's aware of it! I think I heard your friend mention Wyvern Court! Well, that's where *I'm* going.

Undershell (excitedly). You—*you* are going to Wyvern Court! Why, then, you must be——

[*He checks himself.*

His Fellow Passenger. What were you going to say; *what* must I be?

Undershell (to himself). There is no doubt about it; bright, independent girl; gloves a trifle worn; travels second-class for economy; it must be Miss Mull herself; her letter mentioned Lady Culverin as her aunt. A poor relation, probably. She doesn't suspect that I am—— I won't reveal myself just yet; better let it dawn upon her gradually. (*Aloud.*) Why, I was only about to say, why then you must be going to the same house as I am. How extremely fortunate a coincidence!

His Fellow Passenger. That remains to be seen. (*To herself.*) What a funny little man; such a flowery way of talking for a footman. Oh, but I forgot; he said he *wasn't* going to wear livery. Well, he *would* look a sight in it!

PART V

CROSS PURPOSES

In a First-class Compartment.

Lady Maisie (to herself). Poets don't seem to have much self-possession. He seems perfectly overcome by hearing my name like that. If only he doesn't lose his head completely and say something about my wretched letter!

Spurrell (to himself). I'd better tell 'em before they find out for themselves. (*Aloud; desperately.*) My lady, I—I feel I ought to explain at once how I come to be going down to Wyvern like this.

[Lady MAISIE *only just suppresses a terrified protest.*

Lady Cantire (benignly amused). My good sir, there's not the slightest necessity ; I am perfectly aware of who you are, and everything about you !

Spurrell (*incredulously*). But really I don't see *how* your ladyship—— Why, I haven't said a *word* that——

Lady Cantire (*with a solemn waggishness.*) Celebrities who mean to preserve their *incognito* shouldn't allow their friends to see them off. I happened to hear a certain *Andromeda* mentioned, and that was quite enough for Me!

Spurrell (*to himself, relieved*). She knows; seen the sketch of me in the *Dog Fancier*, I expect; goes in for breeding bulls herself, very likely. Well, that's a load off my mind! (*Aloud.*) You don't say so, my lady. I'd no idea your ladyship would have any taste that way; most agreeable surprise to me, I can assure you!

Lady Cantire. I see no reason for *surprise* in the matter. I have always endeavoured to cultivate my taste in all directions; to keep in touch with every modern development. I make it a rule to read and see *everything*. Of course, I have no time to give more than a rapid glance at most things; but I hope some day to be able to have another look at your *Andromeda*. I hear the most glowing accounts from all the judges.

Spurrell (*to himself*). She knows all the judges! She *must* be in the fancy! (*Aloud.*) Any time your ladyship likes to name I shall be proud and happy to bring her round for your inspection.

Lady Cantire (with condescension). If you are kind enough to offer me a copy of *Andromeda,* I shall be *most* pleased to possess one.

Spurrell (to himself). Sharp old customer, this; trying to rush me for a pup. *I* never offered her one! *(Aloud.)* Well, as to *that,* my lady, I've promised so many already, that really I don't—but there—I'll see what I can *do* for you. I'll make a note of it; you mustn't mind having to *wait* a bit.

Lady Cantire (raising her eyebrows). I will make an effort to support existence in the meantime.

Lady Maisie (to herself). I couldn't have believed that the man who could write such lovely verses should be so--well, not *exactly* a gentleman! How *petty* of me to have such thoughts. Perhaps geniuses never *are.* And as if it *mattered!* And I'm sure he's very natural and simple, and I shall like him when I know him better.   [*The train slackens.*

Lady Cantire. What station is this? Oh, it *is* Shuntingbridge. *(To* SPURRELL, *as they get out.)* Now, if you'll kindly take charge of these bags, and go and see whether there's anything from Wyvern to meet us—you will find us here when you come back.

On the Platform at Shuntingbridge.

Lady Cantire. Ah, *there* you are, Phillipson! Yes, you can take the jewel-case; and now you had better go and see after the trunks. (PHILLIPSON *hurries back to the luggage-van;* SPURRELL *returns.*) Well, Mr.—I always forget names, so I shall call you ' Andromeda "—have you found out—— The omnibus, is it? Very well, take us to it, and we'll get in. [*They go outside.*

Undershell (at another part of the platform—to himself). Where has Miss Mull disappeared to? Oh, there she is, pointing out her luggage. What a quantity she travels with! Can't be such a *very* poor relation. How graceful and collected she is, and how she orders the porters about! I really believe I shall enjoy this visit. (*To a porter.*) That's mine—the brown one with a white star. I want it to go to Wyvern Court—Sir Rupert Culverin's.

Porter (shouldering it). Right, sir. Follow me, if you please. [*He disappears with it.*

Undershell (to himself). I mustn't leave Miss Mull alone. (*Advancing to her.*) Can I be of any assistance?

Phillipson. It's all done now. But you might try
and find out how we're to get to the Court.

> [UNDERSHELL *departs; is requested to produce
> his ticket, and spends several minutes in
> searching every pocket but the right one.*

In the Station Yard at Shuntingbridge.

Lady Cantire (*from the interior of the Wyvern
omnibus, testily, to* Footman). What are we waiting
for *now?* Is my maid coming with us—or how?

Footman. There's a fly ordered to take her, my
lady.

Lady Cantire (*to* SPURRELL, *who is standing below*).
Then it's *you* who are keeping us!

Spurrell. If your ladyship will excuse me. I'll just
go and see if they've put out my bag.

Lady Cantire (*impatiently*). Never mind about
your bag.   (*To* Footman.) What have you done
with this gentleman's luggage?

Footman. Everything for the Court is on top now,
my lady.   [*He opens the door for* SPURRELL.

Lady Cantire (*to* SPURRELL, *who is still irresolute*).
For goodness' sake don't hop about on that step!
Come in, and let us start.

Lady Maisie. Please get in—there's plenty of room!

Spurrell (*to himself*). They *are* chummy, and no

SEARCHING EVERY POCKET BUT THE RIGHT ONE.

mistake! (*Aloud, as he gets in.*) I do hope it won't be considered any intrusion—my coming up along with your ladyships, I mean!

Lady Cantire (*snappishly*). Intrusion! I never heard such nonsense! Did you expect to be asked to run behind? You really mustn't be so ridiculously modest. As if your *Andromeda* hadn't procured you the *entrée* everywhere! [*The omnibus starts.*

Spurrell (*to himself*). Good old Drummy! No idea I was such a swell. I'll keep my tail up. Shyness ain't one of *my* failings. (*Aloud, to an indistinct mass at the further end of the omnibus, which is unlighted.*) Er—hum—pitch dark night, my lady, don't get much idea of the country! (*The mass makes no response.*) I was saying, my lady, it's too dark to—— (*The mass snores peacefully.*) Her ladyship seems to be taking a snooze on the quiet, my lady. (*To* Lady MAISIE.) (*To himself.*) Not that *that's* the term for it!

Lady Maisie (*distantly*). My mother gets tired rather easily. (*To herself.*) It's really too dreadful; he makes me hot all over! If he's going to do this kind of thing at Wyvern! And I'm more or less responsible for him, too! I *must* see if I can't—— It will be only kind. (*Aloud, nervously.*) Mr.— Mr. Blair!

Spurrell. Excuse me, my lady, not *Blair*—Spurrell.

Lady Maisie. Of course, *how* stupid of me. I knew it wasn't *really* your name. Mr. *Spurrell*, then, you —you won't mind if I give you just one little hint, *will* you?

Spurrell. I shall take it kindly of your ladyship, whatever it is.

Lady Maisie (*more nervously still*). It's really such a trifle, but—but, in speaking to mamma or me, it isn't at all necessary to say "my lady" or "your ladyship." I—I mean, it sounds rather, well— *formal*, don't you know!

Spurrell (*to himself*). She's going to be chummy now! (*Aloud.*) I thought, on a first acquaintance, it was only manners.

Lady Maisie. Oh—manners? yes, I—I dare say— but still—but still—*not* at Wyvern, don't you know. If you like, you can call mamma "Lady Cantire," and me "Lady Maisie," now and then, and, of course, my aunt will be "Lady Culverin," but—but if there are other people staying in the house, you needn't call them *anything*, do you see?

Spurrell (*to himself*). I'm not likely to have the chance! (*Aloud.*) Well, if you're sure they won't *mind* it, because I'm not used to this sort of thing,

E

so I put myself entirely in your hands,—for, of course, *you* know what brought me down here?

Lady Maisie (to herself). He means my foolish letter! Oh, I must put a stop to *that* at once! (*In a hurried undertone.*) Yes—yes; I—I think I do I mean, I *do* know—but—but *please* forget it—*indeed*, you must!

Spurrell (to himself). Forget I've come down as a vet? The Culverins will take care I don't forget that! (*Aloud.*) But, I say, it's all very well; but how *can* I? Why, look here; I was told I was to come down here on purpose to——

Lady Maisie (on thorns). I know—you needn't tell me! And *don't* speak so loud! *Mamma* might hear!

Spurrell (puzzled). What if she did? Why, I thought her la—your mother *knew!*

Lady Maisie (to herself). He actually thinks I should tell mamma! Oh, how *dense* he is! (*Aloud.*) Yes—yes—of *course* she knows—but—but you might *wake* her! And—and please don't allude to it again —to me or—or any one. (*To herself.*) That I should have to beg him to be silent like this! But what can I *do?* Goodness only knows *what* he mightn't say, if I don't warn him!

Spurrell (nettled). I don't mind *who* knows. *I'm*

not ashamed of it, Lady Maisie—whatever you may be!

Lady Maisie (to herself, exasperated). He dares to imply that *I*'ve done something to be ashamed of! (*Aloud, haughtily.*) I'm *not* ashamed—why *should* I be? Only—oh, can't you *really* understand that—that one may do things which one wouldn't care to be reminded of publicly? I don't *wish* it—isn't *that* enough?

Spurrell (to himself). I see what she's at now—doesn't want it to come out that she's travelled down here with a vet! (*Aloud, stiffly.*) A lady's wish is enough for *me* at any time. If you're sorry for having gone out of your way to be friendly, why, I'm not the person to take advantage of it. I hope I know how to behave. [*He takes refuge in offended silence.*

Lady Maisie (to herself). Why did I say anything at all! I've only made things worse—I've let him see that he *has* an advantage. And he's certain to use it sooner or later—unless I am civil to him. I've offended him now—and I shall *have* to make it up with him!

Spurrell (to himself). I thought all along she didn't seem as chummy as her mother—but to turn round on me like this!

Lady Cantire (waking up). Well, Mr. Andromeda,

I should have thought you and my daughter might have found *some* subject in common ; but I haven't heard a word from either of you since we left the station.

Lady Maisie (to herself). That's *some* comfort! (*Aloud.*) You must have had a nap, mamma. We —we *have* been talking.

Spurrell. Oh yes, we *have* been talking, I can assure you, Lady Cantire !

Lady Cantire. Dear me. Well, Maisie, I hope the conversation was entertaining ?

Lady Maisie. M—most entertaining, mamma !

Lady Cantire. I'm quite sorry I missed it. (*The omnibus stops.*) Wyvern at last ! But *what* a journey it's been, to be sure !

Spurrell (to himself). I should just think it had. I've never been so taken up and put down in all my life ! But it's over now ; and, thank goodness, I'm not likely to see any more of 'em !

[*He gets out with alacrity.*

PART VI

In the Entrance Hall at Wyvern.

Tredwell (*to* Lady CANTIRE). This way, if you please, my lady. Her ladyship is in the Hamber Boudwore.

Lady Cantire. Wait. (*She looks round.*) What has become of that young Mr. Androm——? (*Perceiving* SPURRELL, *who has been modestly endeavouring to efface himself.*) Ah, *there* he is! Now, come along, and be presented to my sister-in-law. She'll be enchanted to know you!

Spurrell. But indeed, my lady, I—I think I'd better wait till she sends for me.

Lady Cantire. Wait? Fiddlesticks! What! A famous young man like you! Remember *Andromeda*, and don't make yourself so ridiculous!

Spurrell (*miserably*). Well, Lady Cantire, if her

ladyship *says* anything, I hope you'll bear me out
that it wasn't——

Lady Cantire. Bear you out? My good young
man, you seem to need somebody to bear you *in!*
Come, you are under *my* wing. *I* answer for your
welcome—so do as you're told.

Spurrell (to himself, as he follows resignedly). It's
my belief there'll be a jolly row when I *do* go in;
but it's not my fault!

Tredwell (opening the door of the Amber Boudoir).
Lady Cantire and Lady Maisie Mull. (*To* SPURRELL.)
What name, if you please, sir?

Spurrell (dolefully). You can say " James Spurrell "
—you needn't *bellow* it, you know!

Tredwell (ignoring this suggestion). Mr. James
Spurrell.

Spurrell (to himself, on the threshold). If I don't
get the chuck for this, I *shall* be surprised, that's all!
[*He enters.*

In a Fly.

Undershell (to himself). Alone with a lovely girl,
who has no suspicion, as yet, that I am the poet
whose songs have thrilled her with admiration!
Could any situation be more romantic? I think I
must keep up this little mystification as long as
possible.

"WHAT NAME, IF YOU PLEASE, SIR?"

Phillipson (*to herself*). I wonder who he is? *Somebody's* Man, I suppose. I do believe he's struck with me. Well, I've no objection. I don't see why I shouldn't forget Jim now and then—he's quite forgotten me! (*Aloud.*) They might have sent a decent carriage for us instead of this ramshackle old summerhouse. We shall be *hours* getting to the house at this rate!

Undershell (*gallantly*). For my part, I care not how long we may be. I feel so unspeakably content to be where I am.

Phillipson (*disdainfully*). In this mouldy, lumbering old concern? You must be rather easily contented, then!

Undershell (*dreamily*). It travels only too swiftly. To me it is a veritable enchanted car, drawn by a magic steed.

Phillipson. I don't know whether he's magic—but I'm sure he's lame. And stuffiness is not *my* notion of *enchantment.*

Undershell. I'm not prepared to deny the stuffiness. But cannot you guess what has transformed this vehicle for me—in spite of its undeniable shortcomings — or must I speak more plainly still?

Phillipson. Well, considering the shortness of our

acquaintance, I must say you've spoken quite plainly enough as it is!

Undershell. I know I must seem unduly expansive, and wanting in reserve ; and yet that is not my true disposition. In general, I feel an almost fastidious shrinking from strangers——.

Phillipson (*with a little laugh*). Really? I shouldn't have thought it!

Undershell. Because, in the present case, I do not —I cannot—feel as if we *were* strangers. Some mysterious instinct led me, almost from the first, to associate you with a certain Miss Maisie Mull.

Phillipson. Well, I wonder how you discovered *that.* Though you shouldn't have said " Miss "— *Lady* Maisie Mull is the proper form.

Undershell (*to himself*). Lady Maisie Mull! I attach no meaning to titles—and yet nothing but rank could confer such perfect ease and distinction. (*Aloud.*) I should have said *Lady* Maisie Mull, undoubtedly—forgive my ignorance. But at least I have divined you. Does nothing tell you who and what *I* may be?

Phillipson. Oh, I think I can give a tolerable guess at what *you* are.

Undershell. You recognize the stamp of the Muse upon me, then?

Phillipson. Well, I shouldn't have taken you for a *groom* exactly.

Undershell (with some chagrin). You are really too flattering!

Phillipson. Am I? Then it's your turn now. You might say you'd never have taken me for a *lady's maid!*

Undershell. I might—if I had any desire to make an unnecessary and insulting remark.

Phillipson. Insulting? Why, it's what I *am!* I'm maid to Lady Maisie. I thought your mysterious instinct told you all about it?

Undershell (to himself—after the first shock). A lady's maid! Gracious Heaven! What have I been saying—or rather, what *haven't* I? (*Aloud.*) To— to be sure it did. Of course, I quite understand that. (*To himself.*) Oh, confound it all, I wish we were at Wyvern!

Phillipson. And, after all, you've never told me who *you* are. Who *are* you?

Undershell (to himself). I must not humiliate this poor girl! (*Aloud.*) I? Oh—a very insignificant person, I assure you! (*To himself.*) This is an occasion in which deception is pardonable—even justifiable!

Phillipson. Oh, I knew *that* much. But you let

out just now you had to do with a Mews. You
aren't a rough-rider, are you?

Undershell. N—not *exactly*—not a *rough*-rider.
(*To himself.*) Never on a horse in my life!—unless
I count my *Pegasus.* (*Aloud.*) But you are right
in supposing I am connected with a muse—in one
sense.

Phillipson. I said so, didn't I? Don't you think
it was rather clever of me to spot you, when you're
not a bit horsey-looking?

Undershell (*with elaborate irony*). Accept my compliments on a power of penetration which is simply
phenomenal!

Phillipson (*giving him a little push*). Oh, go along
—it's all talk with you—I don't believe you mean
a word you say!

Undershell (*to himself*). She's becoming absolutely
vulgar. (*Aloud.*) I don't—I *don't;* it's a manner
I have; you mustn't attach any importance to it—
none whatever!

Phillipson. What! Not to all those high-flown
compliments? Do you mean to tell me you are
only a gay deceiver, then?

Undershell (*in horror*). Not a *deceiver*, no; and
decidedly not *gay.* I mean I *did* mean the *compliments*, of course. (*To himself.*) I mustn't let her

suspect anything, or she'll get talking about it; it would be too horrible if this were to get round to Lady Maisie or the Culverins—so undignified; and it would ruin all my *prestige!* I've only to go on playing a part for a few minutes, and—maid or not —she's a most engaging girl!

> [*He goes on playing the part, with the un-expected result of sending* Miss PHILLIP-SON *into fits of uncontrollable laughter.*

At a Back Entrance at **Wyvern.** *The Fly has just set down* PHILLIPSON *and* UNDERSHELL.

Tredwell (receiving PHILLIPSON). Lady Maisie's maid, I presume? I'm the butler here—Mr. Tred-well. Your ladies arrived some time back. I'll take you to the housekeeper, who'll show you their rooms, and where yours is, and I hope you'll find everything comfortable. (*In an undertone, indicating* UNDERSHELL, *who is awaiting recognition in the door-way.*) Do you happen to know who it is *with* you?

Phillipson (in a whisper). I can't quite make him out—he's so flighty in his talk. But he *says* he belongs to some Mews or other.

Tredwell. Oh, then *I* know who he is. We expect him right enough. He's a partner in a crack firm of

Vets. We've sent for him special. I'd better see
to him, if you don't mind finding your own way to
the housekeeper's room, second door to the left,
down that corridor. (PHILLIPSON *departs.*) Good
evening to you, Mr.—ah—Mr.—— ?

Undershell (*coming forward*). Mr. Undershell.
Lady Culverin expects me, I believe.

Tredwell. Quite correct, Mr. Undershell, sir. She
do. Leastwise, I shouldn't say myself she'd require
to see you—well, not *before* to-morrow morning—
but you won't mind *that*, I dare say.

Undershell (*choking*). Not mind that! Take me
to her at once!

Tredwell. Couldn't take it on myself, sir, really.
There's no particular 'urry. I'll let her ladyship
know you're 'ere; and if she wants you, she'll send
for you; but, with a party staying in the 'ouse, and
others dining with us to-night, it ain't likely as
she'll have time for you till to-morrow.

Undershell. Oh, then whenever her ladyship
should find leisure to recollect my existence, will
you have the goodness to inform her that I have
taken the liberty of returning to town by the next
train?

Tredwell. Lor! Mr. Undershell, you aren't so
pressed as all *that*, are you? I know my lady

wouldn't like you to go without seeing you person-
ally ; no more wouldn't Sir Rupert. And I understood you was coming down for the Sunday !

Underwell (*furious*). So did *I*—but not to be
treated like this !

Tredwell (*soothingly*). Why, *you* know what ladies
are. And you couldn't see Deerfoot—not properly,
to-night, either.

Undershell. I have seen enough of this place
already. I intend to go back by the next train, I
tell you.

Tredwell. But there *ain't* any next train up to-
night—being a loop line—not to mention that I've
sent the fly away, and they can't spare no one at the
stables to drive you in. Come, sir, make the best of
it. I've had my horders to see that you're made
comfortable, and Mrs. Pomfret and me will expect
the pleasure of your company at supper in the
'ousekeeper's room, 9.30 sharp. I'll send the
steward's room boy to show you to your room.

[*He goes, leaving* UNDERSHELL *speechless.*

Undershell (*almost foaming*). The insolence of
these cursed aristocrats ! Lady Culverin will see
me when she has time, forsooth ! I am to be enter-
tained in the servants' hall ! *This* is how our upper
classes honour Poetry ! I won't stay a single hour

under their infernal roof. I'll walk. But where
to?   And how about my luggage?

[PHILLIPSON *returns.*

Phillipson. Mr. Tredwell says you want to go
already! It *can't* be true! Without even waiting
for supper?

Undershell (*gloomily*). Why should I wait for
supper in this house?

Phillipson. Well, *I* shall be there; I don't know
if *that's* any inducement.   [*She looks down.*

Undershell (*to himself*). She is a singularly bewitching creature; and I'm starving. Why *shouldn't*
I stay—if only to shame these Culverins? It will
be an experience—a study in life. I can always go
afterwards. I *will* stay. (*Aloud.*) You little know
the sacrifice you ask of me, but enough; I give way.
We shall meet—(*with a gulp*)—in the housekeeper's
room!

Phillipson (*highly amused*). You *are* a comical
little man. You'll be the death of me if you go on
like that!   [*She flits away.*

Undershell (*alone*). I feel disposed to be the death
of *somebody!* Oh, Lady Maisie Mull, to what a
bathos have you lured your poet by your artless
flattery—a banquet presided over by your aunt's
butler!

PART VII

IGNOTUM PRO MIRIFICO

The Amber Boudoir at Wyvern immediately after Lady CANTIRE *and her daughter have entered.*

Lady Cantire (in reply to Lady CULVERIN). Tea? oh yes, my dear; anything *warm!* I'm positively perished—that tedious cold journey and the long drive afterwards! I always tell Rupert he would see me *far* oftener at Wyvern if he would only get the company to bring the line round close to the park gates, but it has *no* effect upon him! (*As* TREDWELL *announces* SPURRELL, *who enters in trepidation.*) Mr. James Spurrell! Who's Mr.——? Oh, to be sure; *that's* the name of my interesting young poet—*Andromeda,* you know, my dear! Go and be pleasant to him, Albinia, he wants reassuring.

Lady Culverin (a trifle nervous). How do you do, Mr.—ah—Spurrell? (*To herself.*) I *said* he ended in "'ell"! (*Aloud.*) So pleased to see you! We think so much of your *Andromeda* here, you know. Quite delightful of you to find time to run down !

Spurrell (*to himself*). Why, *she's* chummy, too! Old Drummy pulls me through everything ! (*Aloud.*) Don't name it, my la—hum—Lady Culverin. No trouble at all ; only too proud to get your summons !

Lady Culverin (*to herself*). He doesn't seem very revolutionary ! (*Aloud.*) That's so sweet of you; when so many must be absolutely fighting to get you !

Spurrell. Oh, as for that, there *is* rather a run on me just now, but I put everything else aside for *you*, of course !

Lady Culverin (*to herself*). He's soon *reassured*. (*Aloud, with a touch of frost.*) I am sure we must consider ourselves most fortunate. (*Turning to the* Countess.) You *did* say cream, Rohesia? Sugar, Maisie dearest ?

Spurrell (*to himself*). I'm all right up to now ! I suppose I'd better say nothing about the horse till *they* do. I feel rather out of it among these nobs, though. I'll try and chum on to little Lady Maisie again; she may have got over her temper by this time, and she's the only one I know. (*He approaches her.*) Well, Lady Maisie, here I *am*, you see. I'd really no idea your aunt would be so friendly ! I

F

say, you know, you don't mind *speaking* to a fellow, do you? I've no one else I can go to—and—and it's a bit strange at first, you know!

Lady Maisie (colouring with mingled apprehension, vexation, and pity). If I can be of any help to you, Mr. Spurrell—— !

Spurrell. Well, if you'd only tell me what I ought to *do!*

Lady Maisie. Surely that's very simple; do *nothing;* just take everything quietly as it comes, and you *can't* make any mistakes.

Spurrell (anxiously). And you don't think anybody 'll see anything out of the way in my being here like this?

Lady Maisie (to herself). I'm only too afraid they *will!* (*Aloud.*) You really *must* have a little self-confidence. Just remember that no one here could produce anything a millionth part as splendid as your *Andromeda!* It's *too* distressing to see you so appallingly humble! (*To herself.*) There's Captain Thicknesse over there—he *might* come and rescue me; but he doesn't seem to care to!

Spurrell. Well, you *do* put some heart into me, Lady Maisie. I feel equal to the lot of 'em now!

Pilliner (to Miss Spelwane). Is *that* the poet? Why, but I say—he's a *fraud!* Where's his matted head? He's not a bit ragged, or rusty either. And why don't he dabble? Don't seem to know what to do with his hands quite, though, *does* he?

Miss Spelwane (*coldly*). He knows how to do some very exquisite poetry with *one* of them, at all events. I've been reading it, and *I* think it perfectly marvellous!

Pilliner. I see what it is, you're preparing to turn his matted head for him? I warn you you'll only waste your sweetness. That pretty little Lady Maisie's annexed *him*. Can't you content yourself with *one* victim at a time?

Miss Spelwane. Don't be so utterly idiotic! (*To herself.*) If Maisie imagines she's to be allowed to monopolise the only man in the room worth talking to!——

Captain Thicknesse (*to himself, as he watches* Lady MAISIE). She is lookin' prettier than ever! Forgotten me. Used to be friendly enough once, though, till her mother warned me off. Seems to have a good deal to say to that poet fellow; saw her colour up from here the moment he came near; he's *begun* Petrarchin', hang him! I'd cross over and speak to her if I could catch her eye. Don't know, though; what's the use? She wouldn't thank me for interruptin'. She likes these clever chaps;

don't signify to her if they *are* bounders, I suppose.
I'm not intellectual. Gad, I wish I'd gone back to
Aldershot!

Lady Cantire (by the tea-table). Why don't you
make that woman of yours send you up decent
cakes, my dear? These are cinders. I'm afraid
you let her have too much of her own way. Now,
tell me—who are your party? Vivien Spelwane!
Never have that girl to meet me again, I can't
endure her; and that affected little ape of a Mr.
Pilliner—h'm! Do I see Captain Thicknesse?
Now, I don't object to *him*. Maisie and he used
to be great friends. . . . Ah, how do you *do*, Captain
Thicknesse? Quite pleasant finding you here; such
ages since we saw anything of you! Why haven't
you been near us all this time? . . . Oh, I may
have been out once or twice when you called; but
you might have tried again, *mightn't* you? There,
I forgive you; you had better go and see if you can
make your peace with Maisie!

Captain Thicknesse (to himself, as he obeys). Doosid
odd, Lady Cantire comin' round like this. Wish
she'd thought of it before.

Lady Cantire (in a whisper). He's always been
such a favourite of mine. They tell me his uncle,
poor dear Lord Dunderhead, is *so* ill— felt the loss of

his only son so terribly.   Of course it will make a great difference—in many ways.

Captain Thicknesse (*constrainedly to* Lady MAISIE). How do you do?   Afraid you've forgotten me.

Lady Maisie. Oh no, indeed!   (*Hurriedly.*)   You —you don't know Mr. Spurrell, I think?   (*Introducing them.*)   Captain Thicknesse.

Captain Thicknesse. How are you?   Been hearin' a lot about you lately.   *Andromeda,* don't you know; and that kind of thing.

Spurrell. It's wonderful what a hit she seems to have made—not that I'm *surprised* at it, either; I always knew——

Lady Maisie (*hastily*). Oh, Mr. Spurrell, you haven't had any tea! *Do* go and get some before it's taken away.   [SPURRELL *goes.*

Captain Thicknesse. Been tryin' to get you to notice me ever since you came; but you were so awfully absorbed, you know!

Lady Maisie. Was I?   So absorbed as all that! What with?

Captain Thicknesse. Well, it looked like it—with talkin' to your poetical friend.

Lady Maisie (*flushing*). He is not *my* friend in particular; I—I admire his poetry, of course.

Captain Thicknesse (*to himself*). Can't even speak

of him without a change of colour. Bad sign that!
(*Aloud.*) You always *were* keen about poetry and
literature and that in the old days, weren't you?
Used to rag me for not readin' enough. But I do
now. I was readin' a book only last week. I'll tell
you the name if you give me a minute to think—
book everybody's readin' just now—no end of a
clever book.

[Miss SPELWANE *rushes across to* Lady MAISIE.

Miss Spelwane. Maisie, dear, how are you? You
look *so* tired! That's the journey, I suppose. (*Whispering.*) Do tell me—is that really the author of
Andromeda drinking tea close by? You're a *great*
friend of his, I know. Do be a dear, and introduce
him to me! I declare the dogs have made friends
with him already. Poets have such a wonderful
attraction for animals, haven't they?

[Lady MAISIE *has to bring* SPURRELL *up and*
introduce him ; Captain THICKNESSE
chooses to consider himself dismissed.

Miss Spelwane (with shy adoration). Oh, Mr.
Spurrell, I feel as if I *must* talk to you about
Andromeda. I *did* so admire it!

Spurrell (to himself). Another of 'em! They seem
uncommonly sweet on " bulls " in this house! (*Aloud.*)
Very glad to hear you say so, I'm sure. But I'm

bound to say she's about as near perfection as anything *I* ever—I dare say you went over her points——

Miss Spelwane. Indeed, I believe none of them were lost upon me; but my poor little praise must seem so worthless and ignorant!

Spurrell (*indulgently*). Oh, I wouldn't say *that*. I find some ladies very knowing about these things. I'm having a picture done of her.

Miss Spelwane. Are you really? *How* delightful! As a frontispiece?

Spurrell. Eh? Oh no—full length, and sideways —so as to show her legs, you know.

Miss Spelwane. Her legs? Oh, of *course*—with "her roseal toes cramped." I thought that such a *wonderful* touch!

Spurrell. They're not more cramped than they ought to be; she never turned them *in*, you know!

Miss Spelwane (*mystified*). I didn't suppose she did. And now tell me—if it's not an indiscreet question —when do you expect there'll be another edition?

Spurrell (*to himself*). Another addition! *She's* cadging for a pup now! (*Aloud.*) Oh—er—really —couldn't say.

Miss Spelwane. I'm sure the first must be disposed

of by this time. I shall look out for the next *so*
eagerly!

Spurrell (*to himself*). Time I " off " ed it. (*Aloud.*)
Afraid I can't say anything definite—and, excuse me
leaving you, but I think Lady Culverin is looking
my way.

Miss Spelwane. Oh, by all *means ?*   (*To herself.*)   I
might as well praise a pillar-post ! And after spending quite half an hour reading him up, too!   I
wonder if Bertie Pilliner was right; but I shall have
him all to myself at dinner.

Lady Cantire. And where is Rupert ? too busy of
course to come and say a word!   Well, some day
he may understand what a sister is—when it's too
late.   Ah, here's our nice unassuming young poet
coming up to talk to you.   Don't *repel* him, my
dear !

Spurrell (*to himself*).   Better give her the chance
of telling me what's wrong with the horse, I suppose.
(*Aloud.*)   Er—nice old-fashioned sort of house this,
Lady Culverin. (*To himself.*) I'll work round to
the stabling by degrees.

Lady Culverin (*coldly*). I believe it dates from the
Tudors—if that is what you mean.

Lady Cantire. My dear Albinia, I *quite* understand him ; " old-fashioned " is *exactly* the epithet.

And I was born and brought up here, so perhaps I should know.

> [*A footman enters, and comes up to* SPURRELL *mysteriously.*

Footman. Will you let me have your keys, if you please, sir?

Spurrell (in some alarm). My keys! (*Suspiciously.*) Why, what do you want *them* for?

Lady Cantire (in a whisper). Isn't he *deliciously* unsophisticated? Quite a child of nature! (*Aloud.*) My dear Mr. Spurrell, he wants your keys to unlock your portmanteau and put out your things; you'll be able to dress for dinner all the quicker.

Spurrell. Do you mean—am I to have the honour of sitting down to table with all of *you?*

Lady Culverin (to herself). Oh, my goodness, what *will* Rupert say? (*Aloud.*) Why, of course, Mr. Spurrell; how can you ask?

Spurrell (feebly). I—I didn't know, that was all. (*To* Footman.) Here you are, then. (*To himself.*) Put out my things?—he'll find nothing to put out except a nightgown, sponge bag, and a couple of brushes! If I'd only known I should be let in for this, I'd have brought dress-clothes. But how *could* I? I—I wonder if it would be any good telling 'em quietly how it is. I shouldn't like 'em to think I

"MY KEYS! WHY, WHAT DO YOU WANT THEM FOR?"

hadn't got any. (*He looks at* Lady CANTIRE *and her sister-in-law, who are talking in an undertone.*) No, perhaps I'd better let it alone. I—I can allude to it in a joky sort of way when I come down!

PART VIII

SURPRISES —AGREEABLE AND OTHERWISE

In the Amber Boudoir. Sir RUPERT *has just entered.*

Sir Rupert. Ha, Maisie, my dear, glad to see you! Well, Rohesia, how are you, eh? You're *looking* uncommonly well! No idea you were here!

Spurrell (to himself). Sir Rupert! He'll hoof me out of this pretty soon, I expect!

Lady Cantire (aggrieved). We have been in the house for the best part of an hour, Rupert—as you might have discovered by inquiring—but no doubt you preferred your comfort to welcoming so unimportant a guest as your sister!

Sir Rupert (to himself). Beginning already! (*Aloud.*) Very sorry—got rather wet riding—had to change everything. And I knew Albinia was here.

Lady Cantire (magnanimously). Well, we won't begin to quarrel the moment we meet; and you are forgetting your other guest. (*In an undertone.*) Mr. Spurrell—the poet—wrote *Andromeda*. (*Aloud.*) Mr. Spurrell, come and let me present you to my brother.

Sir Rupert. Ah, how d'ye do? (*To himself, as he shakes hands.*) What the deuce am I to say to this fellow? (*Aloud.*) Glad to see you here, Mr. Spurrell—heard all about you—*Andromeda*, eh? Hope you'll manage to amuse yourself while you're with us; afraid there's not much you can do *now* though.

Spurrell (*to himself*). Horse in a bad way; time they let me see it. (*Aloud.*) Well, we must see, sir; I'll do all *I* can.

Sir Rupert. You see, the shooting's *done* now.

Spurrell (*to himself, professionally piqued*). They might have waited till I'd seen the horse before they shot him! After calling me in like this! (*Aloud.*) Oh, I'm sorry to hear that, Sir Rupert. I wish I could have got here earlier, I'm sure.

Sir Rupert. Wish we'd asked you a month ago, if you're fond of shooting. Thought you might look down on sport, perhaps.

Spurrell (*to himself*). Sport? Why, he's talking of *birds*—not the horse! (*Aloud.*) Me, Sir Rupert? Not *much!* I'm as keen on a day's gunning as any man, though I don't often get the chance now.

Sir Rupert (to himself, pleased). Come, he don't seem strong against the Game Laws! (*Aloud.*) Thought you didn't look as if you sat over your desk all day! There's hunting still, of course. Don't know whether you ride?

Spurrell. Rather so, sir! Why, I was born and bred in a sporting county, and as long as my old uncle was alive, I could go down to his farm and get a run with the hounds now and again.

Sir Rupert (delighted). Capital! Well, our next meet is on Tuesday—best part of the country; nearly all grass, and nice clean post and rails. You must stay over for it. Got a mare that will carry your weight perfectly, and I think I can promise you a run—eh, what do you say?

Spurrell (to himself, in surprise). He *is* a chummy old cock! I'll wire old Spavin that I'm detained on biz; and I'll tell 'em to send my riding-breeches and dress-clothes down! :(*Aloud.*) It's uncommonly kind of you, sir, and I think I can manage to stop on a bit.

Lady Culverin (to herself). Rupert must be out of his senses! It's bad enough to have him here till Monday! (*Aloud.*) We mustn't forget, Rupert, how valuable Mr. Spurrell's time is; it would be too selfish of us to detain him here a day longer than——

Lady Cantire. My dear, Mr. Spurrell has already said he can *manage* it; so we may all enjoy his society with a clear conscience. (Lady CULVERIN *conceals her sentiments with difficulty.*) And now, Albinia, if you'll excuse me, I think I'll go to my room and rest a little, as I'm rather overdone, and you have all these tiresome people coming to dinner to-night.

[*She rises and leaves the room; the other ladies follow her example.*

Lady Culverin. Rupert, I'm going up now with Rohesia. You know where we've put Mr. Spurrell, don't you? The Verney Chamber. [*She goes out.*

Sir Rupert. Take you up now, if you like, Mr. Spurrell—it's only just seven, though. Suppose you don't take an hour to dress, eh?

Spurrell. Oh dear no, sir, nothing like it! (*To himself.*) Won't take me two minutes as I am now! I'd better tell him—I can say my bag hasn't come. I don't believe it *has*, and, anyway, it's a good excuse. (*Aloud.*) The—the fact is, Sir Rupert, I'm afraid that my luggage has been unfortunately left behind.

Sir Rupert. No luggage, eh ? Well, well, it's of no consequence. But I'll ask about it—I dare say it's all right.   [*He goes out.*

Captain Thicknesse (*to* SPURRELL). Sure to have turned up, you know—man will have seen that. Shouldn't altogether object to a glass of sherry and bitters before dinner. Don't know how *you* feel—suppose you've a soul *above* sherry and bitters, though ?

Spurrell. Not at this moment. But I'd soon *put* my soul above a sherry and bitters if I got a chance !

Captain Thicknesse (*after reflection*). I say, you know, that's rather smart, eh ? (*To himself.*) Aw'fly clever sort of chap, this, but not stuck up—not half a bad sort, if he *is* a bit of a bounder. (*Aloud.*) Anythin' in the evenin' paper ? Don't get 'em down here.

Spurrell. Nothing much. I see there's an objection to Monkey-tricks.

Captain Thicknesse (*startled*). No, by Jove ! Hope they'll overrule it—make a lot of difference to me if they don't.

Spurrell. Don't fancy there's much in it. Your money's safe enough, I expect. Have you any particular fancy for the Grand National ? I know something that's safe to win, bar accidents—a dead cert, sir ! Got the tip straight from the stable.

"I SAY, YOU KNOW, THAT'S RATHER SMART, EH?"

G

You just take my advice, and pile all you can on
Jumping Joan.

Captain **Thicknesse** (*later, to himself, after a long
and highly interesting conversation*). Thunderin' clever
chap—never knew poets *were* such clever chaps.
Might be a "bookie," by Gad! No wonder Maisie
thinks such a lot of him! [*He sighs.*

Sir **Rupert** (*returning*). Now, Mr. Spurrell, if
you'll come upstairs with me, I'll show you your
quarters. By the way, I've made inquiries about
your luggage, and I think you'll find it's all right.
(*As he leads the way up the staircase.*) Rather
awkward for you if you'd had to come down to dinner
just as you are, eh?

Spurrell (*to himself*). Oh, lor, my beastly bag *has*
come after all! Now they'll *know* I didn't bring
a dress suit. What an owl I was to tell him!
(*Aloud, feebly.*) Oh—er—very awkward indeed, Sir
Rupert!

Sir **Rupert** (*stopping at a bedroom door*). Verney
Chamber—here you are. Ah, my wife forgot to have
your name put on the door—better do it now, eh?
(*He writes it on the card in the door-plate.*) There—
well, hope you'll find it all comfortable—we dine at
eight, you know. You've plenty of time for all
you've got to do!

Spurrell (*to himself*). If I only knew *what* to do! I shall never have the cheek to come down as I am!

[*He enters the Verney Chamber dejectedly.*

In an Upper Corridor in the East Wing.

Steward's Room Boy (to UNDERSHELL). This is your room, sir—you'll find a fire lit and all.

Undershell (*scathingly*). A fire? For me! I scarcely expected such an indulgence. You are *sure* there's no mistake?

Boy. This is the room I was told, sir. You'll find candles on the mantelpiece, and matches.

Undershell. Every luxury indeed! I am pampered —*pampered!*

Boy. Yes, sir. And I was to say as supper's at ar-past nine, but Mrs. Pomfret would be 'appy to see you in the Pugs' Parlour whenever you pleased to come down and set there.

Undershell. The Pugs' Parlour?

Boy. What we call the 'ousekeeper's room, among ourselves, sir.

Undershell. Mrs. Pomfret does me too much honour. And shall I have the satisfaction of seeing your intelligent countenance at the festive board, my lad?

Boy (*giggling*). On'y to *wait*, sir. I don't set down to meals along with the *upper* servants, sir!

Undershell. And I—a mere man of genius—*do!*
These distinctions must strike you as most arbitrary; but restrain any natural envy, my young friend. I assure you I am not puffed up by this promotion!

Boy. No, sir. (*To himself, as he goes out.*) I believe he's a bit dotty, I do. I don't understand a word he's been a-talking of!

Undershell (*alone, surveying the surroundings*). A cockloft, with a painted iron bedstead, a smoky chimney, no bell, and a text over the mantelpiece! Thank Heaven, that fellow Drysdale can't see me here! But I will not sleep in this place, my pride will only just bear the strain of staying to supper— no more. And I'm hanged if I go down to the housekeeper's room till hunger drives me. It's not eight yet—how shall I pass the time? Ha, I see they've favoured me with pen and ink. I will invoke the Muse. Indignation should make verses, as it did for Juvenal; and *he* was never set down to sup with slaves! [*He writes.*

In the Verney Chamber.

Spurrell (*to himself*). My word, what a room! Carpet hung all over the walls, big fourposter, carved ceiling, great fireplace with blazing logs,—if this is

how they do a *vet* here, what price the *other* fellows'
rooms? And to think I shall have to do without
dinner, just when I was getting on with 'em all so
swimmingly! I *must*. I can't, for the credit of the
profession—to say nothing of the firm—turn up in a
monkey jacket and tweed bags, and that's all *I've*
got except a nightgown! . . . It's all very well for
Lady Maisie to say, "Take everything as it comes,"
but if she was in *my* fix! . . . And it isn't as if
I hadn't *got* dress things either. If only I'd brought
'em down, I'd have marched in to dinner as cool as
a—— (*he lights a pair of candles.*) Hullo! What's
that on the bed? (*He approaches it.*) Shirt! white
tie! socks! coat, waistcoat, trousers—they *are* dress
clothes! . . . And here's a pair of brushes on the
table! I'll swear they're not *mine*—there's a mono-
gram on them—"U.G." What does it all mean?
Why, of course! regular old trump, Sir Rupert, and
naturally he wants me to do him credit. He saw
how it was, and he's gone and rigged me out! In
a house like this, they're ready for emergencies—
keep all sizes in stock, I dare say. . . . It isn't
"U.G." on the brushes—it's "G.U."—"Guest's Use."
Well, this is what I call doing the thing in style!
Cinderella's nothing to it! Only hope they're a
decent fit. (*Later, as he dresses.*) Come, the shirt's

all right; trousers a trifle short—but they'll let
down; waistcoat—whew, must undo the buckle—
hang it, it *is* undone! I feel like a hooped barrel in
it! Now the coat—easy does it. Well, it's *on ;* but
I shall have to be peeled like a walnut to get it off
again. . . . Shoes? ah, here they are—pair of
pumps. Phew—must have come from the Torture
Exhibition in Leicester Square; glass slippers nothing
to 'em! But they'll have to do at a pinch; and
they *do* pinch like blazes! Ha, ha, that's good! I
must tell that to the Captain. (*He looks at himself
in a mirror.*) Well, I can't say they're up to mine
for cut and general style; but they're passable. And
now I'll go down to the drawing-room and get on
terms with all the smarties!

　　　[*He saunters out with restored complacency.*

PART IX

In the Chinese Drawing-room at Wyvern. TIME—
7.50. *Lady* CULVERIN *is alone, glancing over a
written list.*

Lady Cantire (entering). Down already, Albinia?
I *thought* if I made haste I should get a quiet chat
with you before anybody else came in. What is
that paper? Oh, the list of couples for Rupert.
May I see? (*As* Lady CULVERIN *surrenders it.*) My
dear, you're *not* going to inflict that mincing little
Pilliner boy on poor Maisie! That really *won't do*.
At least let her have somebody she used to. Why
not Captain Thicknesse? He's an old friend, and
she's not seen him for months. I must alter that,
if you've no objection. (*She does.*) And then you've
given my poor poet to that Spelwane girl! Now,
why ?

Lady Culverin. I thought she wouldn't mind putting up with him just for one evening.

Lady Cantire. Wouldn't *mind !* Putting up with him ! And is that how you speak of a celebrity when you are so fortunate as to have one to entertain ? *Really,* Albinia !

Lady Culverin. But, my dear Rohesia, you must allow that, whatever his talents may be, he is not— well, not *quite* one of Us. Now, *is* he ?

Lady Cantire (blandly). My dear, I never heard he had any connection with the manufacture of chemical manures, in which your worthy papa so greatly distinguished himself—if *that* is what you mean.

Lady Culverin (with some increase of colour). That is *not* what I meant, Rohesia—as you know perfectly well. And I do say that this Mr. Spurrell's manner is most objectionable ; when he's not obsequious, he's horribly familiar !

Lady Cantire (sharply). I have not observed it. He strikes me as well enough—for that class of person. And it is intellect, soul, all that kind of thing that *I* value. I look *below* the surface, and I find a great deal that is very original and charming in this young man. And surely, my dear, if I find myself able to associate with him, *you* need not be so fastidious! I consider him my *protégé*, and I won't have him slighted. He is far too good for Vivien Spelwane!

Lady Culverin (with just a suspicion of malice). Perhaps, Rohesia, you would like him to take *you* in?

Lady Cantire. That, of course, is quite out of the question. I see you have given me the Bishop— he's a poor, dry stick of a man—never forgets he was the Headmaster of Swisham—but he's always glad to meet *me*. I freshen him up so.

Lady Culverin. I really don't know whom I *can* give Mr. Spurrell. There's Rhoda Cokayne, but she's not poetical, and she'll get on much better with Archie Bearpark. Oh, I forgot Mrs. Brooke-Chatteris—she's sure to *talk*, at all events.

Lady Cantire (as she corrects the list). A lively, agreeable woman—she'll amuse him. *Now* you can give Rupert the list.

> [Sir RUPERT *and various members of the house-party appear one by one;* Lord *and* Lady LULLINGTON, *the* Bishop of BIRCHESTER *and* Mrs. RODNEY, Mr. *and* Mrs. EARWAKER, *and* Mr. SHORTHORN *are announced at intervals; salutations, recognitions, and commonplaces are exchanged.*

Lady Cantire (later—to the Bishop, *genially*). Ah, my dear Bishop, you and I haven't met since we had our great battle about—now, was it the necessity of throwing open the Public Schools to the lower classes—for whom of course they were originally *intended*—or was it the failure of the Church to reach the working man? I really forget.

The Bishop (who has a holy horror of the Countess). I—ah—fear I cannot charge my memory so precisely, my dear Lady Cantire. We—ah—differ unfortunately on so many subjects. I trust, however, we may—ah—agree to suspend hostilities on this occasion?

Lady Cantire (with even more bonhomie). Don't be too sure of *that*, Bishop. I've several crows to pluck with you, and we are to go in to dinner together, you know!

The Bishop. Indeed? I had no conception that such a pleasure was in store for me! (*To himself.*) This must be the penance for breaking my rule of never dining out on Saturday! Severe—but not unmerited!

Lady Cantire. I wonder, Bishop, if you have seen this wonderful volume of poetry that every one is talking about—*Andromeda?*

The Bishop (conscientiously). I chanced only this

morning, by way of momentary relaxation, to take
up a journal containing a notice of that work, with
copious extracts. The impression left on my mind
was—ah—unfavourable; a certain talent, no doubt,
some felicity of expression, but a noticeable lack of
the—ah—reticence, the discipline, the—the scholarly
touch which a training at one of our great Public
Schools (I forbear to particularise), and at a
University, can alone impart. I was also pained
to observe a crude discontent with the existing
Social System—a system which, if not absolutely
perfect, cannot be upset or even modified without
the gravest danger. But I was still more distressed
to note in several passages a decided taint of the
morbid sensuousness which renders so much of our
modern literature sickly and unwholesome.

Lady Cantire. All prejudice, my dear Bishop;
why, you haven't even *read* the book! However,
the author is staying here now, and I feel con-
vinced that if you only knew him, you'd alter your
opinion. Such an unassuming, inoffensive creature!
There, he's just come in. I'll call him over
here. . . . Goodness, why does he shuffle along in
that way!

Spurrell (meeting Sir RUPERT). Hope I've kept
nobody waiting for *me,* Sir Rupert. (*Confidentially.*)

I'd rather a job to get these things on; but they're really a wonderful fit, considering!

[*He passes on, leaving his host speechless.*

Lady Cantire. That's right, Mr. Spurrell. Come here, and let me present you to the Bishop of Birchester. The Bishop has just been telling me he considers your *Andromeda* sickly, or unhealthy, or something. I'm sure you'll be able to convince him it's nothing of the sort.

[*She leaves him with the* Bishop, *who is visibly annoyed.*

Spurrell (*to himself, overawed*). Oh, Lor! Wish I knew the right way to talk to a Bishop. Can't call him nothing—so doosid familiar. (*Aloud.*) *Andromeda* sickly, your—(*tentatively*)—your Right Reverence? Not a bit of it—sound as a roach!

The Bishop. If I had thought my—ah—criticisms were to be repeated—I might say misrepresented, as the Countess has thought proper to do, Mr. Spurrell, I should not have ventured to make them. At the same time, you must be conscious yourself, I think, of certain blemishes which would justify the terms I employed.

Spurrell. I never saw any in *Andromeda* myself, your—your Holiness. You're the first to find a fault in her. I don't say there mayn't be something

"I'D RATHER A JOB TO GET THESE THINGS ON; BUT THEY'RE REALLY A
WONDERFUL FIT, CONSIDERING!"

dicky about the setting and the turn of the tail, but that's a trifle.

The Bishop. I did not refer to the setting of the tale, and the portions I object to are scarcely trifles. But pardon me if I prefer to end a discussion that can hardly be other than unprofitable. (*To himself, as he turns on his heel.*) A most arrogant, self-satisfied, and conceited young man—a truly lamentable product of this half-educated age!

Spurrell (*to himself*). Well, he may be a dab at dogmas—he don't know much about dogs. Drummy's got a constitution worth a dozen of *his!*

Lady Culverin (*approaching him*). Oh, Mr. Spurrell, Lord Lullington is most anxious to know you. If you will come with me. (*To herself, as she leads him up to Lord* LULLINGTON.) I do *wish* Rohesia wouldn't force me to do this sort of thing!

[*She presents him.*

Lord Lullington (*to himself*). I suppose I *ought* to know all about his novel, or whatever it is he's done. (*Aloud, with courtliness.*) Very pleased to make your acquaintance, Mr. Spurrell; you've—ah —delighted the world by your *Andromeda.* When are we to look for your next production? Soon, I hope.

Spurrell (*to himself*). He's after a pup now!

Never met such a doggy lot in my life! (*Aloud.*)
Er—well, my lord, I've promised so many as it is,
that I hardly see my way to——

Lord Lullington (*paternally*). Take my advice, my
dear young man, leave yourself as free as possible.
Expect you to give us your best, you know.

> [*He turns to continue a conversation.*

Spurrell (*to himself*). Give it! He won't get it
under a five-pound note, I can tell him. (*He makes
his way to* Miss SPELWANE.) I say, what do you
think the old Bishop's been up to? Pitching into
Andromeda like the very dooce—says she's *sickly!*

Miss Spelwane (*to herself*). He brings his literary
disappointments to *me*, not Maisie! (*Aloud, with
the sweetest sympathy.*) How dreadfully unjust!
Oh, I've dropped my fan—no, pray don't trouble;
I can pick it up. My arms are so long, you know
—like a kangaroo's—no, what *is* that animal which
has such long arms? You're so clever, you *ought* to
know!

Spurrell. I suppose you mean a gorilla?

Miss Spelwane. How crushing of you! But you
must go away now, or else you'll find nothing to
say to me at dinner—you take me in, you know.
I hope you feel privileged. *I* feel—— But if I told
you, I might make you too conceited!

Spurrell (*gracefully*). Oh, it's not so easily done as all *that*!

[Sir RUPERT. *approaches with* Mr. SHORTHORN.

Sir Rupert. Vivien, my dear, let me introduce Mr. Shorthorn—Miss Spelwane. (*To* SPURRELL.) Let me see—ha—yes, you take in Mrs. Chatteris. Don't know her? Come this way, and I'll find her for you.   [*He marches* SPURRELL *off*.

Mr. Shorthorn (*to* Miss SPELWANE). Good thing getting this rain at last; a little more of this dry weather and we should have had no grass to speak of!

Miss Spelwane (*who has not quite recovered from her disappointment*). And now you *will* have some grass to speak of? *How* fortunate!

Spurrell (*as dinner is announced, to* Lady MAISIE). I say, Lady Maisie, I've just been told I've got to take in a married lady. *I* don't know what to talk to her about. I should feel a lot more at home with you. Couldn't we work it somehow?

Lady Maisie (*to herself*). What a fearful suggestion —but I simply *daren't* snub him! (*Aloud.*) I'm afraid, Mr. Spurrell, we must both put up with the partners we have; most distressing, isn't it—*but!*

[*She gives a little shrug*.

Captain Thicknesse (*immediately behind her, to himself*). Gad, *that's* pleasant! I knew I'd better have gone to Aldershot! (*Aloud.*) I've been told off to take you in, Lady Maisie—not *my* fault, don't you know.

Lady Maisie. There's no need to be so apologetic about it. (*To herself.*) Oh, I *hope* he didn't hear what I said to that wretch!

Captain Thicknesse. Well, I rather thought there *might* be, perhaps.

Lady Maisie (*to herself*). He *did* hear it. If he's going to be so stupid as to misunderstand, I'm sure *I* shan't explain.

> [*They take their place in the procession to the dining-hall.*

PART X

BORROWED PLUMES

In UNDERSHELL'S *Bedroom in the East Wing at*
Wyvern.
TIME—*About* 9 P.M.

The Steward's Room Boy (*knocking and entering*).
Brought you up some 'ot water, sir, case you'd like
to clean up afore supper.

Undershell. I presume evening dress is not indis-
pensable in the housekeeper's room; but I can hardly
make even the simplest toilet until you are good
enough to bring up my portmanteau. Where is it?

Boy. I never 'eard nothink of no porkmanteau,
sir!

Undershell. You will hear a good deal about it,
unless it is forthcoming at once. Just find out what's
become of it—a new portmanteau, with a white star
painted on it.

[*The* Boy *retires, impressed. An interval.*

Boy (reappearing). I managed to get a few words with Thomas, our second footman, just as he was coming out o' the 'all, and *he* sez the only porkmanteau with a white star was took up to the Verney Chamber, which Thomas unpacked it hisself.

Undershell. Then tell Thomas, with my compliments, that he will trouble himself to pack it again immediately.

Boy. But Thomas has to wait at table, and besides, he says as he laid out the dress things, and the gen'lman as is in the Verney Chamber is a wearin' of 'em now, sir.

Undershell (indignant). But they're *mine!* Confound his impudence! Here, I'll write him a line at once. (*He scribbles a note.*) There, see that the gentleman of the Verney Chamber gets this at once, and bring me his answer.

Boy. What! *me* go into the dinin'-'all, with all the swells at table? I dursn't. I should get the sack from old Treddy.

Undershell. I don't care who takes it so long as it *is* taken. Tell Thomas it's *his* mistake, and he must do what he can to put it right. Say I shall certainly complain if I don't get back my clothes and portmanteau. Get that note delivered somehow, and I'll give you half-a-crown. (*To himself, as the* Boy *departs, much against his will.*) If Lady Culverin doesn't consider me fit to appear at her dinner-table, I don't see why my evening clothes should be more privileged!

In the Dining-hall.   The table is oval ; SPURRELL *is placed between* Lady RHODA COKAYNE *and* Mrs. BROOKE-CHATTERIS.

Mrs. Chatteris (*encouragingly, after they are seated*). Now, I shall expect you to be very brilliant and entertaining. *I'*ll do all the listening for once in a way—though, generally, I can talk about all manner of silly things with *anybody !*

Spurrell (*extremely ill at ease*). Oh—er—I should say you were quite equal to *that.* But I really can't think of anything to talk *about.*

Mrs. Chatteris. That's a bad beginning. I always find the *menu* cards such a good subject, when there's anything at all out of the common about them. If they're ornamented, you *can* talk about them— though not for *very* long at a time, don't you think ?

Spurrell (*miserably*). I can't say how long I could go on about *ornamented* ones—but these are plain. (*To himself.*) I can hear this waistcoat going already—and we're only at the soup!

Mrs. Chatteris. It *is* a pity. Never mind; tell me

about literary and artistic people. Do you know, I'm rather glad I'm not literary or artistic myself; it seems to make people so *queer-looking,* somehow. Oh, of course I didn't mean *you* looked queer—but *generally,* you know. You've made quite a success with your *Andromeda,* haven't you? I only go by what I'm told—I don't read much myself. We women have so many really serious matters to attend to—arranging about dinners, and visits, and trying on frocks, and then rushing about from party to party. I so seldom get a quiet moment. Ah, I knew I wanted to ask you something. Did you ever know any one called Lady Grisoline?

Spurrell. Lady—er—Grisoline? No; can't say I do. I know Lady Maisie, that's all.

Mrs. Chatteris. Oh, and *she* was the original? Now, that *is* exciting! But I should hardly have recognised her—"lanky," you know, and "slanting green eyes." But I suppose you see everybody differently from other people? It's having so much imagination. I dare say *I* look green or something to you now—though really I'm *not.*

Spurrell (to himself). I don't understand more than about half she's saying. (*Aloud.*) Oh, I don't see anything particularly green about *you.*

Mrs. Chatteris (only partially pleased). I wonder if

you meant that to be complimentary—no, you needn't explain. Now, tell me, is there any news about the Laureateship? Who's going to get it? Will it be Swinburne or Lewis Morris?

Spurrell (*to himself*). Never heard of the stakes or the horses either. (*Aloud.*) Well, to tell you the truth, I haven't been following their form—too many of these small events nowadays.

Mrs. Chatteris (*to herself*). It's quite amusing how jealous these poets are of one another! (*Aloud.*) Is it true they get a butt of sherry given them for it?

Spurrell. I've heard of winners getting a bottle or two of champagne in a bucket—not sherry. But a little stimulant won't hurt a crack when he comes in, provided it's not given him too soon ; wait till he's got his wind and done blowing, you know.

Mrs. Chatteris. I'm taking that in. I know it's very witty and satirical, and I dare say I shall understand it in time.

Spurrell. Oh, it doesn't matter much if you don't. (*To himself.*) Pleasant kind of woman—but a perfect fool to talk to !

Mrs. Chatteris (*to herself*). I've always *heard* that clever writers are rather stupid when you meet them —it's quite true.

Captain Thicknesse (*to himself*). I should like her

to see that I've got some imagination in me, though she *does* think me such an ass. (*Aloud, to* Lady Maisie.) Jolly old hall this is, with the banners, and the gallery, and that—makes you fancy some of those old mediæval Johnnies in armour—knights, you know—comin' clankin' in and turnin' us all out.

Lady Maisie (to herself). I do trust Mr. Spurrell isn't saying something too dreadful. I'm sure I heard my name just now. (*Aloud, absently, to* Captain Thicknesse.) No, did you *really?* How amusing it must have been!

Captain Thicknesse (aggrieved). If you'd done me the honour of payin' any attention to what I was sayin', you'd have found out it *wasn't* amusin'.

Lady Maisie (starting). Oh, *wasn't* it? I'm so sorry I missed it. I—I'm afraid I was thinking of something else. Do tell me again!

Captain Thicknesse (still hurt). No, I won't inflict it on you—not worth repeatin'. And I should only be takin' off your attention from a fellow that *does* know how to talk.

Lady Maisie (with a guiltiness which she tries to carry off under dignity). I don't think I understand what you mean.

Captain Thicknesse. Well, I couldn't help hearin'

what you said to your poet-friend before we went in about having to put up with partners; and it isn't what you may call flattering to a fellow's feelin's, being put up with.

Lady Maisie (*hotly*). It—it was not intended for you. You entirely misunderstood!

Captain Thicknesse. Dare say I'm very dense; but, even to *my* comprehension, it's plain enough that the reason why you weren't listenin' to me just now was that the poet had the luck to say somethin' that you found more interesting.

Lady Maisie. You are *quite* wrong—it's too absurd; I never even met Mr. Spurrell in my life till this afternoon. If you really *must* know, I heard him mention my name, and—and I wondered, naturally, what he could possibly be saying.

Captain Thicknesse. Somethin' very charmin', and poetical, and complimentary, I'm sure, and I'm makin' you lose it all. Apologise—shan't happen again.

Lady Maisie. Please be sensible, and let us talk of something else. Are you staying here long?

Captain Thicknesse. You will be gratified to hear I leave for Aldershot to-morrow. Meant to have gone to-day. Sorry I *didn't* now.

Lady Maisie. I think it was a thousand pities you

didn't, as you seem to have stayed on purpose to be as stupid and unkind as you possibly can.

[*She turns to her other neighbour,* Lord LUL-LINGTON.

Mrs. Chatteris (*to* Captain THICKNESSE, *who is on her other side*). Oh, Captain Thicknesse, what *do* you think Mr. Spurrell has just told me? You remember those lines to Lady Grisoline that Mr. Pilliner made such fun of this morning? Well, they were meant for Lady Maisie! They're quite old friends, it seems. *So* romantic! Wouldn't you like to know how they came to meet?

Captain Thicknesse. Can't say I'm particularly curious—no affair of mine, don't you know. (*To himself.*) And she told me they'd never met before! Sooner I get back the better. Only in the way here.

Lady Maisie (*turning to him*). Well, are you as determined to be as disagreeable as ever? Oh yes, I see you are!

Captain Thicknesse. I'm hurt, that's what it is, and I'm not clever at hiding my feelin's. Fact is, I've just been told somethin' that—well, it's no business of *mine*, only you *might* have been a little more frank with an old friend, instead of leavin' it to come through somebody else. These things always come out, you know.

Lady Maisie (to herself). That wretch *has* been talking! I knew he would! (*Aloud.*) I—I know I've been very foolish.. If I was to tell you some time——

Captain Thicknesse (hastily). Oh, no reason why you should tell me anything. Assure you, I—I'm not curious.

Lady Maisie. In that case I shall certainly not trouble you. (*To herself.*) He may think just what he pleases, *I* don't care. But, oh, if Mr. Spurrell dares to speak to me after this, I shall astonish him!

Lady Rhoda (to SPURRELL). I say—I *am* in a funk. Only just heard who I'm next to. I always do feel such a perfect fool when I've got to talk to a famous person—and you're *frightfully* famous, aren't you?

Spurrell (modestly). Oh, I don't know—I suppose I *am*, in a sort of way, through *Andromeda.* Seem to think so *here*, anyhow.

Lady Rhoda. Well, I'd better tell you at once, I'm no good at poetry—can't make head or tail of it, some'ow. It does seem to me such—well, such footle. Awf'ly rude of me sayin' things like that!

Spurrell. Is it? I'm just the same—wouldn't give a penny a yard for poetry, myself!

Lady Rhoda. You wouldn't? I *am* glad. *Such* a let-off for me! I was afraid you'd want to talk of

"IT DOES SEEM TO ME SUCH—WELL, SUCH FOOTLE."

nothin' else, and the only things I can really talk
about are horses and dogs, and that kind of thing.

Spurrell. That's all right, then.   All I don't know
about dogs and horses you could put in a homœo-
pathic globule—and *then* it would rattle!

Lady Rhoda. Then you're just the man.   Look
here, I've an Airedale at home, and he's losin' all his
coat and——   [*They converse with animation.*

Spurrell (*later—to himself*). I am getting on.   I
always knew I was made for Society.   If only this
coat was easier under the arms!

Thomas (*behind him—in a discreet whisper*). Beg
your pardon, sir, but I was requested to 'and you
this note, and wait for an answer.

Spurrell (*opening it, and reading*). "Mr. Galfrid
Undershell thinks that the gentleman who is occupy-
ing the Verney Chamber has, doubtless by inadver-
tence, put on Mr. Undershell's evening clothes.   As
he requires them immediately, he will be obliged by
an early appointment being made, with a view to
their return." (*To himself.*)   Oh, Lor!   Then it
wasn't Sir Rupert, after all!   Just when I was
beginning to enjoy my evening, too.   What on earth
am I to say to this chap?   I *can't* take 'em all off
here!

[*He sits staring at the paper in blank dismay.*

PART XI

In the Dining-hall.

Spurrell (to himself, uncomfortably conscious of the expectant THOMAS *in his rear).* Must write *something* to this beggar, I suppose ; it'll keep him quiet. (*To* Mrs. BROOKE-CHATTERIS.) I—I just want to write a line or two. Could you oblige me with a lead pencil ?

Mrs. Chatteris. You are really going to write ! At a dinner-party, of all places ! Now *how* delightfully original and unconventional of you ! I promise not to interrupt till the inspiration is over. Only, really, I'm afraid I don't carry lead pencils about with me— so bad for one's frocks, you know !

Thomas (in his car). I can lend you a pencil, sir, if you require one.

[*He provides him with a very minute stump.*

Spurrell (*reading what he has written on the back of* UNDERSHELL'S *missive*). "Will be in my room (Verney Chamber) as soon after ten as possible.

"J. SPURRELL."

(*He passes the paper to* THOMAS *surreptitiously.*) There, take him that.   [THOMAS *retires.*

Archie (*to himself.*) The calm cheek of these writin' chaps! I saw him takin' notes under the table! Lady Rhoda ought to know the sort of fellow he is—and she shall! (*To* Lady RHODA, *in an aggrieved undertone.*) I should advise you to be jolly careful what you say to your other neighbour; he's takin' it all down. I just caught him writin'. He'll be bringing out a satire, or whatever he calls it, on us all by and bye—you see if he won't!

Lady Rhoda. What an ill-natured boy you are! Just because *he* can write, and you *can't.* And I don't believe he's doing anythin' of the sort. I'll ask him—*I* don't care! (*Aloud, to* SPURRELL.) I say, I know I'm awfully inquisitive—but I do want to know so—you've just been writin' notes or somethin', haven't you? Mr. Bearpark declares you're goin' to take them all off here—you're not really, *are* you?

Spurrell (*to himself*). That sulky young chap has spotted it! (*Aloud, stammering.*) I—take everything off? *Here!* I—I assure you I should never even *think* of doing anything so indelicate!

Lady Rhoda. I was sure that was what you'd say! But still (*with reviving uneasiness*), I suppose you *have* made use of things that happened just to fit your purpose, haven't you?

Spurrell (*penitently*). All I can say is, that—if I have—you won't catch me doing it *again!* And other people's things *don't* fit. I'd much rather have my own.

Lady Rhoda (*relieved*). Of course! But I'm glad you told me. (*To* ARCHIE, *in an undertone.*) I *asked* him—and, as usual, you were utterly wrong. So you'll please not to be a pig!

Archie (*jealously*). And you're goin' to go on talkin' to him all through dinner? Pleasant for me —when I took you down!

Lady Rhoda. You want to be taken down yourself, I think. And I mean to talk to him if I choose. You can talk to Lady Culverin—she likes boys! (*Turning to* SPURRELL.) I was goin' to ask you— ought a schipperke to have meat? Mine won't touch puppy biscuits.

> [SPURRELL *enlightens her on this point*; ARCHIE
> *glowers.*

Lady Cantire (*perceiving that the* Bishop *is showing*

signs of restiveness). Well, Bishop, I wish I could find you a little more ready to listen to what the other side has to say!

The Bishop (who has been "heckled" to the verge of his endurance.) I am—ah—not conscious of any unreadiness to enter into conversation with the very estimable lady on my other side, should an opportunity present itself.

Lady Cantire. Now, that's one of your quibbles, my dear Bishop, and I detest quibbling! But at least it shows you haven't a leg to stand upon.

The Bishop. Precisely—nor to—ah—run away upon, dear lady. I am wholly at your mercy, you perceive!

Lady Cantire (triumphantly). Then you *admit* you're beaten? Oh, I don't despair of you *yet*, Bishop.

The Bishop. I confess I am less sanguine. (*To himself.*) Shall I have strength to bear these buffets with any remains of Christian forbearance through three more courses? Ha, thank Heaven, the salad!

[*He cheers up at the sight of this olive-branch.*

Mrs. Earwaker (to PILLINER). Now, I don't altogether approve of the New Woman myself; but still, I am glad to see how women are beginning to assert themselves and come to the front; surely you sympathise with all that?

Pilliner (plaintively). No, really I *can't*, you know! I'd so much rather they *wouldn't*. They've made us poor men feel positively obsolete! They'll snub us out of existence soon—our sex will be extinct—and then they'll be sorry. There'll be nobody to protect them from one another! After all, we can't help being what we are. It isn't *my* fault that I was born a Man Thing—now, *is* it?

Lady Cantire (overhearing this remark). Well, if it *is* a fault, Mr. Pilliner, we must all acknowledge that you've done everything in your power to correct it!

Pilliner (sweetly). How nice and encouraging of you, dear Lady Cantire, to take up the cudgels for me like that!

> [Lady CANTIRE *privately relieves her feelings by expressing a preference for taking up a birch rod, and renews her attack on the* Bishop.

Mr. Shorthorn (who has been dragging his mental depths for a fresh topic—hopefully, to Miss SPELWANE). By the bye, I haven't asked you what you thought about these—er—revolting daughters?

Miss Spelwane. No, you haven't; and I thought it *so* considerate of you.

> Mr. SHORTHORN *gives up dragging, in discouragement.*

I

Pilliner (*sotto voce, to* Miss SPELWANE). Have you quite done sitting on that poor unfortunate man ? *I* heard you !

Miss Spelwane (*in the same tone*). I'm afraid I *have* been rather beastly to him. But, oh, he *is* such a bore—he *would* talk about his horrid "silos," till I asked him whether they would eat out of his hand. After that, the subject dropped—somehow.

Pilliner. I see you've been punishing him for not happening to be a distinguished poet. I thought *he* was to have been the fortunate man ?

Miss Spelwane. So he was; but they changed it all at the last moment; it really was rather provoking. I *could* have talked to *him*.

Pilliner. Lady Rhoda appears to be consoling him. Poor dear old Archie's face is quite a study. But really I don't see that his poetry is so very wonderful; no more did *you* this morning !

Miss Spelwane. Because you deliberately picked out the worst bits, and read them as badly as you could !

Pilliner. Ah, well, he's here to read them for himself now. I dare say he'd be delighted to be asked.

Miss Spelwane. Do you know, Bertie, that's rather a good idea of yours. I'll ask him to read us something to-night.

Pilliner (aghast). **To-night!** With all these people here? I say, they'll never *stand* it, you know.

[Lady CULVERIN *gives the signal.*

Miss Spelwane (as she rises). They ought to feel it an immense privilege. I know *I* shall.

The Bishop (to himself, as he rises). Port in sight —at last! But, oh, *what* I have had to suffer!

Lady Cantire (at parting). Well, we've had quite one of our old discussions. I always enjoy talking to *you*, Bishop. But I haven't *yet* got at your reasons for voting as you did on the Parish Councils Bill; we must go into that upstairs.

The Bishop (with strict veracity). I shall be—ah—all impatience, Lady Cantire. (*To himself.*) I fervently trust that a repetition of this experience may yet be spared me!

Lady Rhoda (as she leaves SPURRELL). You will tell me the name of the stuff upstairs, won't you? So very much ta!

Archie (to himself). I'd like to tar him very much, and feather him too, for cuttin' me out like this! (*The men sit* **down**; SPURRELL *finds himself between* ARCHIE *and* Captain THICKNESSE, *at the further end of the table;* ARCHIE *passes the wine to* SPURRELL *with a scowl.*) What are you drinkin'? Claret? What do you do your writin' on, now, as a general thing?

"I SHALL BE—AH—ALL IMPATIENCE, LADY CANTIRE."

Spurrell (*on the defensive*). On paper, sir, when I've any to do. Do you do yours on a *slate?*

Captain Thicknesse. I say, that's rather good. Had you there, Bearpark!

Spurrell (*to* ARCHIE, *lowering his voice*). Look here, I see you're trying to put a spoke in my wheel. You saw me writing at dinner, and went and told that young lady I was going to take everything off there and then, which you must have known I wasn't likely to do. Now, sir, it's no business of yours that I can see ; but, as you seem to be interested, I may tell you that I shall go up and do it in my own room, as soon as I leave this table, and there will be no fuss or publicity about it whatever. I hope you're satisfied now?

Archie. Oh, *I'm* satisfied. (*He rises.*) Left my cigarette-case upstairs—horrid bore—must go and get it.

Captain Thicknesse. They'll be bringing some round in another minute.

Archie. Prefer my own. (*To himself, as he leaves the hall.*) I knew I was right. That bounder *is* meaning to scribble some rot about us all! He's goin' straight up to his room to do it. . . . Well, he may find a little surprise when he gets there!

Captain Thicknesse (*to himself*). Mustn't let this

poet fellow think I'm jealous; dare say, after all,
there's nothing serious between them. Not that it
matters to me; any way, I may as well talk to him.
I wonder if he knows anything about steeplechasin'.

> [*He discovers that* SPURRELL *is not unacquainted
> with this branch of knowledge.*

In a Corridor leading to the Housekeeper's Room.
TIME—9.30 P.M.

Undershell (*to himself*). If I wasn't absolutely
compelled by sheer hunger, I would not touch a
morsel in this house. But I can't get my things
back till after ten. As soon as ever I do, I will
insist on a conveyance to the nearest inn. In the
meantime I must sup. After all, no one need know
of this humiliating adventure. And if I *am* compelled to consort with these pampered menials, I
think I shall know how to preserve my dignity—
even while adapting myself to their level. And that
girl will be there—a distinctly redeeming fact in the
situation. I will be easy—affable, even; I will lay
aside all foolish pride; it would be unreasonable to
visit their employer's snobbery upon their unoffend-
ing heads. I hear conversation inside this room.
This must be the door. I—I suppose I had better
go in.   [*He enters.*

PART XII

DIGNITY UNDER DIFFICULTIES

In the Housekeeper's Room at Wyvern; Mrs. POMFRET,
*the Housekeeper, in a black silk gown and her
smartest cap, is seated in a winged armchair by
the fire, discussing domestic politics with* LADY
CULVERIN'S *maid,* Miss STICKLER. *The Chef,*
M. RIDEVOS, *is resting on the sofa, in languid
converse with* Mlle. CHIFFON, Miss SPELWANE'S
maid; PILLINER'S *man,* LOUCH, *watches* STEPTOE,
Sir RUPERT'S *valet, with admiring envy, as he
makes himself agreeable to* Miss PHILLIPSON, *who
is in demi-toilette, as are all the other ladies' maids
present.*

Miss Stickler (in an impressive undertone). All I
do say, Mrs. Pomfret, ma'am, is this: if that girl
Louisa marches into the pew to-morrow, as she did
last Sunday, before the second laundry maid—and

her only under-scullery maid—such presumptious-
ness should be put a stop to in future!

Mrs. Pomfret (wheezily). Depend upon it, my dear,
it's her ignorance; but I shall most certainly speak
about it. Girls must be taught that ranks was made
to be respected, and the precedency into that pew
has come down from time immemoriable, and is not
to be set aside by such as her while *I*'m 'ousekeeper
here.

Mlle. Chiffon (in French, to M. RIDEVOS). You
have the air fatigued, my poor friend! Oh, there—
but fatigued!

M. Ridevos. Broken, Mademoiselle, absolutely
broken. But what will you? This night I surpass
myself. I achieve a masterpiece—a sublime pyramid
of quails with a sauce that will become classic. I
pay now the penalty of a veritable crisis of nerves.
It is of my temperament as artist.

Mlle. Chiffon. And me, my poor friend, how I have
suffered from the cookery of these others—I who
have the stomach so feeble, so fastidious! Figure
to yourself an existence upon the villainous curry,
the abominable "Iahristue," beloved by these bar-
barians, but which succeed with me not at all—oh,
but not at all! Since I am here—ah, the difference!
I digest as of old—I am gay. But next week to

"BROKEN, MADEMOISELLE, ABSOLUTELY BROKEN."

return with mademoiselle to the curry, my poor friend, what regrets!

M. Ridevos. For me, dear mademoiselle, for me the regrets—to hear no more the conversation, so spiritual, so sympathetic, of a fellow-countrywoman. For remark that here they are stupid—they comprehend not. And the old ones they roll at me the eyes to make terror. Behold this Gorgon who approaches. She adores me, my word of honour, this ruin!

[*Miss* STICKLER *comes up to the sofa smiling in happy unconsciousness.*

Miss Stickler (graciously). So you've felt equal to joining us for once, Mossoo! We feel it a very 'igh compliment, I can assure you. We've really been feeling quite 'urt at the way you keep to yourself —you might be a regular 'ermit for all *we* see of you!

M. Ridevos. For invent, dear Mees, for create, ze arteeste must live ze solitaire as of rule. To-night— no! I emairge, as you see, to res-tore myself viz your smile.

Miss Stickler (flattered). Well, I've always said, Mossoo, and I always *will* say, that for polite 'abits and pretty speeches, give *me* a Frenchman!

M. Ridevos (alarmed). For me it is too moch 'appiness. For anozzer, ah!

[*He kisses his fingers with ineffable grace.*

Phillipson (*advancing to meet* Miss DOLMAN, *who has just entered*). Why, I'd no idea I should meet *you* here, Sarah! And how have you been getting on, dear? Still with—— ?

Miss Dolman (*checking her with a look*). Her grace? No, we parted some time ago. I'm with Lady Rhoda Cokayne at present. (*In an undertone, as she takes her aside.*) You needn't say anything here of your having known me at Mrs. Dickenson's. I couldn't afford to have it get about in the circle I'm in that I'd ever lived with any but the nobility. I'm sure you see what I mean. Of course I don't mind your saying we've *met*.

Phillipson. Oh, I *quite* understand. I'll say nothing. I'm obliged to be careful myself, being maid to Lady Maisie Mull.

Miss Dolman. My *dear* Emma! It *is* nice seeing you again—such *friends* as we used to be!

Phillipson. At her Grace's? I'm afraid you're thinking of somebody else. (*She crosses to* Mrs. POMFRET.) Mrs. Pomfret, what's become of the gentleman I travelled down with—the horse doctor? I do hope he means to come in; he would amuse you, Mr. Steptoe. I never heard anybody go on like him; he *did* make me laugh so!

Mrs. Pomfret. I really can't say *where* he is, my

dear. I sent up word to let him know he was welcome here whenever he pleased; but perhaps he's feeling a little shy about coming down.

Phillipson. Oh, I don't think he suffers much from *that.* (*As the door opens.*) Ah, *there* he is!

Mrs. Pomfret (*rising, with dignity, to receive* UNDERSHELL, *who enters in obvious embarrassment*). Come in, sir. I'm glad to see you've found your way down at last. Let me see, I haven't the advantage of knowing your—Mr. Undershell, *to* be sure! Well, Mr. Undershell, we're very pleased to see you. I hope you'll make yourself quite at home. Her ladyship gave particular directions that we was to look after you—*most* particular she was!

Undershell. You are very good, ma'am. I am obliged to Lady Culverin for her (*with a gulp*) condescension. But I shall not trespass more than a short time upon your hospitality.

Mrs. Pomfret. Don't speak of it as trespassing, sir. It's not often we have a gentleman of your profession as a visitor, but you are none the less welcome. Now I'd better introduce you all round, and then you won't feel yourself a stranger. Miss Phillipson you *have* met, I know.

[*She introduces him to the others in turn;* UNDERSHELL *bows helplessly.*

Steptoe (*with urbanity*). Your fame, sir, has preceded you. And you'll find us a very friendly and congenial little circle on a better acquaintance—if this is your first experience of this particular form of society ?

Undershell (*to himself*). I mustn't be stiff, I'll put them at their ease. (*Aloud.*) Why, I must admit, Mr. Steptoe, that I have never before had the privilege of entering the—(*with an ingratiating smile all round him*) the " Pugs' Parlour," as I understand you call this very charming room.

[*The company draw themselves up and cough in disapprobation.*

Steptoe (*very stiffly*). Pardon *me*, sir, you have been totally misinformed. Such an expression is not current *here*.

Mrs. Pomfret (*more stiffly still*). It is never alluded to in *my* presence except as the 'ousekeeper's room, which is the right and proper name for it. There may be some other term for it in the servants' 'all for anything *I* know to the contrary—but, if you'll excuse me for saying so, Mr. Undershell, we'd prefer for it not to be repeated in *our* presence.

Undershell (*confusedly*). I—I beg ten thousand pardons. (*To himself.*) To be pulled up like this for trying to be genial—it's really *too* humiliating!

Steptoe (*relaxing*). Well, well, sir; we must make some allowances for a neophyte. You'll know better another time, *I* dare say. Miss Phillipson here has been giving you a very favourable character as a highly agreeable rattle, Mr. Undershell. I hope we may be favoured with a specimen of your social talents later on. We're always grateful here for anything in that way—such as a recitation now, or a comic song, or a yumorous imitation—anything, in short, calculated to promote the general harmony and festivity will be appreciated.

Miss Stickler (*acidly*). Provided it is free from any helement of coarseness, which we do *not* encourage— far from it!

Undershell (*suppressing his irritation*). You need be under no alarm, madam. I do not propose to attempt a performance of *any* kind.

Phillipson. Don't be so solemn, Mr. Undershell! I'm sure you can be as comical as any play-actor when you choose!

Undershell. I really don't know how I can have given you that impression. If you expect me to treat my lyre like a *horse-collar*, and grin through it, I'm afraid I am unable to gratify you.

Steptoe (*at sea*). Capital, sir, the professional allusion very neat. You'll come out presently, *I* can see, when supper's on the table. Can't expect you to rattle till you've something *inside* of you, can we?

Miss Stickler. Reelly, Mr. Steptoe, I *am* surprised at such commonness from *you!*

Steptoe. Now you're too severe, Miss Stickler, you are indeed. An innocent little Judy Mow like that!

Tredwell (outside). Don't answer *me*, sir. Ham I butler 'ere, or ham I *not?* I've a precious good mind to report you for such a hignorant blunder. . . . I don't want to hear another word about the gentleman's cloes—you'd no hearthly business for to do such a thing at all! (*He enters and flings himself down on a chair.*) That Thomas is beyond everything—stoopid *hass* as he is!

Mrs. Pomfret (concerned). La, Mr. Tredwell, you *do* seem put out! Whatever have Thomas been doing *now?*

Undershell (to himself). It's really very good of him to take it to heart like this! (*Aloud.*) Pray don't let it distress you; it's of no consequence, none at all!

Tredwell (glaring). I'm the best judge of that, Mr. Undershell, sir—if you'll allow *me*; *I* don't call my porogatives of no consequence, whatever *you* may! And that feller Thomas, Mrs. Pomfret, actially 'ad the hordacity, without consulting me previous, to go and 'and a note to one of our gentlemen at the hupstairs table, all about some hassinine mistake he'd made with his cloes! What call had he to take it upon himself? I feel puffecly disgraced that such a thing should have occurred under my authority!

> [*The* Steward's Room Boy *has entered with a dish, and listens with secret anxiety on his own account.*

Undershell. I assure you there is no harm done. The gentleman is wearing my evening clothes—but he's going to return them——

> [*The conclusion of the sentence is drowned in a roar of laughter from the majority.*

Tredwell (*gasping*). Hevenin' cloes! *Your* hevenin'—— P'raps you'll 'ave the goodness to explain yourself, sir!

Steptoe. No, no, Tredwell, my dear fellah, you don't understand our friend here—he's a bit of a wag, don't you see? He's only trying to pull your leg, that's all; and, Gad, he did it too! But you mustn't take liberties with *this* gentleman, Mr. Undershell; he's an important personage *here*, I can tell you!

Undershell (*earnestly*). But I never meant — if you'll only let me explain——

> [*The* Boy *has come behind him, and ad-
> ministers a surreptitious kick, which*
> UNDERSHELL *rightly construes as a hint
> to hold his tongue.*

Tredwell (*in solemn offence*). I'm accustomed, Mr. Hundershell, to be treated in this room with respect and deference—especially by them as come here in the capacity of guests. *From* such I regard any attempt to pull my leg as in hindifferent taste—to say the least of it. I wish to 'ave no more words on the subjick, which is a painful one, and had better be dropped, for the sake of all parties. Mrs. Pomfret, I see supper is on the table, so, by your leave, we had better set down to it.

Phillipson (*to* UNDERSHELL). Never mind *him*, pompous old thing! It *was* awfully cheeky of you, though. You can sit next *me* if you like.

Undershell (*to himself, as he avails himself of this permission*). I shall only make things worse if I explain now. But, oh, great Heavens, *what* a position for a poet!

K

PART XIII

WHAT'S IN A NAME?

At the Supper-table in the Housekeeper's Room. Mrs.
POMFRET *and* TREDWELL *are at the head and
foot of the table respectively.* UNDERSHELL *is
between* Mrs. POMFRET *and* Miss PHILLIPSON.
The Steward's Room Boy *waits.*

Tredwell. I don't see Mr. Adams here this evening, Mrs. Pomfret. What's the reason of that?

Mrs. Pomfret. Why, he asked to be excused to-
night, Mr. Tredwell. You see some of the visitors'
coachmen are putting up their horses here, and he's
helping Mr. Checkley entertain them. (*To* UNDER-
SHELL.) Mr. Adams is our stud-groom, and him
and Mr. Checkley, the 'ed coachman, are very
friendly just now. Adams is very clever with his
horses, I believe, and I'm sure he'd have liked a talk
with you; it's a pity he's engaged elsewhere this
evening.

Undershell (*mystified*). I—I'm exceedingly sorry to have missed him, ma'am. (*To himself.*) Is the stud-groom *literary,* I wonder? . . . Ah, no, I remember now; I allowed Miss Phillipson to conclude that my tastes were equestrian. Perhaps it's just as well the stud-groom *isn't* here!

Mrs. Pomfret. Well, he *may* drop in later on. I shouldn't be surprised if you and he had met before.

Undershell (*to himself*). *I* should. (*Aloud.*) I hardly think it's probable.

Mrs. Pomfret. I've known stranger things than *that* happen. Why, only the other day, a gentleman came into this very room, as it might be yourself, and it struck me he was looking very hard at me, and by and bye he says, " You don't recollect *me,* ma'am, but I know *you* very well," says he. So I said to him, " You certainly have the advantage of me at present, sir." " Well, ma'am," he says, " many years ago I had the honour and privilege of being steward's room boy in a house where you was still-room maid; and I consider I owe the position I have since attained entirely to the good advice you used to give me, as I've never forgot it, ma'am," says he. Then it flashed across me who it was— " Mr. Pocklington!" says I. Which it *were.* And him own man to the Duke of Dumbleshire! Which was what made it so very nice and 'andsome of him to remember me all that time.

Undershell (*perfunctorily*). It must have been most gratifying, ma'am. (*To himself.*) I hope this old lady hasn't any more anecdotes of this highly interesting nature. I mustn't neglect Miss Phillip son—especially as I haven't very long to stay here.

      [*He consults his watch stealthily.*

Miss Phillipson (*observing the action*). I'm sorry you find it so slow here; it's not very polite of you to show it quite so openly though, I must say. [*She pouts.*

Undershell (*to himself*). I can't let this poor girl think me a brute! But I must be careful not to go too far. (*To her, in an undertone which he tries to render unemotional.*) Don't misunderstand me like that. If I looked at my watch, it was merely to count the minutes that are left. In one short half-hour I must go—I must pass out of your life, and you must forget—oh, it will be easy for *you*—but for *me*, ah! you cannot think that I shall carry away a heart entirely unscathed! Believe me, I shall always look back gratefully, regretfully, on——

Phillipson (*bending her head with a gratified little giggle*). I declare you're beginning all that *again*. I never *did* see such a cure as you are.

Undershell (*to himself, displeased*). I wish she could

bring herself to take me a little more seriously. I
can *not* consider it a compliment to be called a
" cure "—whatever that is.

Steptoe (considering it time to interfere). Come,
Mr. Undershell, all this whispering reelly is not fair
on the company! You mustn't hide your bushel
under a napkin like this; don't reserve *all* your
sparklers for Miss Phillipson there.

Undershell (stiffly). I—ah—was not making any
remark that could be described as a sparkler, sir. I
don't sparkle.

Phillipson (demurely). He was being rather sentimental just then, Mr. Steptoe, as it happens. Not
that he can't sparkle, when he likes. I'm sure if
you'd heard how he went on in the fly!

Steptoe (with malice). Not having been privileged
to be present, perhaps our friend here could recollect
a few of his happiest efforts and repeat them.

Miss Dolman. Do, Mr. Undershell, please. I do
love a good laugh.

Undershell (crimson). I—you really must excuse
me. I said nothing worth repeating. I don't
remember that I was particularly——

Steptoe. Pardon me. Afraid I was indiscreet. We
must spare Miss Phillipson's blushes by all manner
of means.

Phillipson. Oh, it was nothing of *that* sort, Mr. Steptoe! *I*'ve no objection to repeat what he said. He called me a little green something or other. No; he said *that* in the train, though. But he would have it that the old cab-horse was a magic steed, and the fly an enchanted chariot; and I don't know what all. (*As nobody smiles.*) It sounded awfully funny as *he* said it, with his face perfectly solemn like it is now, I assure you it did!

Steptoe (*patronisingly*). I can readily believe it. We shall have you contributing to some of our yumerous periodicals, Mr. Undershell, sir, before long. Such facetious talent is too good to be lost, it reelly is.

Undershell (*to himself, writhing*). I gave her credit for more sense. To make me publicly ridiculous like this!   [*He sulks.*

Miss Stickler (*to* M. RIDEVOS, *who suddenly rises*). Mossoo, you're not *going!* Why, whatever's the matter?

M. Ridevos. Pairmeet zat I make my depart. I am cot at ze art.   [*General outcry and sensation.*

Mrs. Pomfret (*concerned*). You never mean that, Mossoo? And a nice dish of quails just put on, too, that they haven't even touched upstairs!

M. Ridevos. It is for zat I do not remmain! Zey 'ave not toch him; my pyramide, result of a genius stupend, énorme! to zem he is nossing; zey retturn him to crash me! To-morrow I demmand zat miladi accept my demission. *Ici je souffre trop!*

[*He leaves the room precipitately.*

Miss Stickler (*offering to rise*). It *does* seem to have upset him! Shall I go after him and see if I can't bring him round?

Mrs. Pomfret (*severely*). Stay where you are, Harriet; he's better left to himself. If he wasn't so wropped up in his cookery, he'd know there's always a dish as goes the round untasted, without why or wherefore. I've no *patience* with the man!

Tredwell (*philosophically*). That's the worst of 'aving to do with Frenchmen; they're so apt to beyave with a sutting childishness that—(*checking himself*)—I really ask your pardon, mamsell, I quite forgot you was of his nationality; though it ain't to be wondered at, I'm sure, for you might pass for an Englishwoman almost anywhere!

Mlle. Chiffon. As you for Frenchman, *hein?*

Tredwell. No, 'ang it *all*, mamsell, I 'ope there's no danger o' *that!* (*To* Miss PHILLIPSON.) Delighted to see the Countess keeps as fit as ever, Miss Phillipson! Wonderful woman for her time o' life! Law, she *did* give the Bishop beans at dinner, and no mistake!

Phillipson. Her ladyship is pretty generous with them to most people, Mr. Tredwell. I'm sure I'd have left her long ago, if it wasn't for Lady Maisie— who *is* a lady, if you like!

Tredwell. She don't favour her ma, I will say *that* for her. By the way, who is the party they brought down with them? a youngish looking chap—seemed a bit out of his helement, when he first come in, though he's soon got over that, judging by the way him and your Lady Rhoda, Miss Dolman, was 'obnobbing together at table!

Phillipson. Nobody came down with *my* ladies; they must have met him in the bus, I expect. What is his name?

Tredwell. Why, he give it to me, I know, when I enounced him; but it's gone clean out of my head again. He's got the Verney Chamber, I know *that* much; but what *was* his name again? I shall forget my own next.

Undershell (involuntarily). In the Verney Chamber? Then the name must be Spurrell!

Phillipson (starting). Spurrell! Why, *I* used to —— But of course it can't be *him!*

Tredwell. Spurrell *was* the name, though. (*With a resentful glare at* UNDERSHELL.) I don't know how *you* came to be aware of it, sir!

Undershell. Why, the fact is, I happened to find out that—(*here he receives an admonitory drive in the back from the* Boy)—that his name *was* Spurrell. (*To himself.*) I wish this infernal boy wouldn't be officious—but perhaps he's right!

Tredwell. Ho, indeed! Well, *another* time, Mr. Hundershell, if you require information about parties staying with *us*, p'raps you'll be good enough to apply to me pussonally, instead of picking it up in some 'ole-and-corner fashion. (UNDERSHELL *controls his indignation with difficulty.*) To return to the individual in question, Miss Phillipson, I should have said myself he was something in the artistic or littery way; he suttingly didn't give me the impression of being a gentleman.

Phillipson (to herself, relieved). Then it *isn't* my Jem! I might have known he wouldn't be visiting here, and carrying on with Lady Rhodas. He'd never forget himself like that—if he *has* forgotten me !

Steptoe. It strikes me he's more of a sporting character, Tredwell. I know when I was circulating with the cigarettes and so on, in the hall just now, he was telling the Captain some anecdote about an old steeplechaser that was faked up to win a selling handicap, and it tickled me to that extent I could hardly hold the spirit-lamp steady.

"HE SITTINGLY DIDN'T GIVE ME THE IMPRESSION OF BEING A GENTLEMAN."

Tredwell. I may be mistook, Steptoe. All *I* can say is, that when me and James was serving cawfy to the ladies in the drawing-room, some of them had got 'old of a little pink book all sprinkled over with silver cutlets, and, rightly *or* wrongly, I took it to 'ave some connection with 'im.

Undershell (*excitedly*). Pink and silver! Might I ask—was it a volume of poetry, called—er—*Andromeda ?*

Tredwell (*crushingly*). That I did not take the liberty of inquiring, sir, as you might be aware if you was a little more familiar with the hetiquette of good society.

> [UNDERSHELL *collapses ;* Mr. ADAMS *enters, and*
> *steps into the chair vacated by the Chef, next*
> *to* Mrs. POMFRET, *with whóm he converses.*

Undershell (*to himself*). To think that they may be discussing my book in the drawing-room at this very moment, while I—I—— (*He chokes.*) Ah, it won't bear thinking of! I must—I *will* get out of this accursed place! I have stood this too long as it is! But I won't go till I have seen this fellow Spurrell, and made him give me back my things. What's the time ? . . . ten ! I can go at last. (*He rises.*) Mrs. Pomfret, will you kindly excuse me ? I—I find I must go at once.

Mrs. Pomfret. Well, Mr. Undershell, sir, you're the best judge; and, if you really can't stop, this is Mr. Adams, who'll take you round to the stables himself, and do anything that's necessary. Won't you, Mr. Adams?

Adams. So you're off to-night, sir, are you? Well, I'd rather ha' shown you Deerfoot by daylight, myself; but there, I dessay that won't make much difference to *you,* so long as you *do* see the 'orse?

Undershell (to himself). So Deerfoot's a *horse!* One of the features of Wyvern, I suppose; they seem very anxious I shouldn't miss it. *I* don't want to see the beast; but I dare say it won't take many minutes; and, if I don't humour this man, I shan't get a conveyance to go away in! (*Aloud.*) No difference whatever—to *me.* I shall be delighted to be shown Deerfoot; only I really can't wait *much* longer; I—I've an appointment elsewhere!

Adams. Right, sir; you get your 'at and coat, and come along with me, and you shall see him at once.

[UNDERSHELL *takes a hasty farewell of* Miss PHILLIPSON *and the company generally— none of whom attempts to detain him—and follows his guide. As the door closes upon them, he hears a burst of stifled merriment, amidst which* Miss PHILLIPSON'S *laughter is only too painfully recognisable.*

PART XIV

LE VÉTÉRINAIRE MALGRÉ LUI

Outside the Stables at Wyvern.
TIME—*About* 10 P.M.

Undershell (to himself, as he follows ADAMS). Now is my time to arrange about getting away from here. (*To* ADAMS.) By the bye, I suppose you can let me have a conveyance of some sort—after I've seen the horse? I—I'm rather in a hurry.

Adams. You'd better speak to Mr. Checkley about that, sir; it ain't in *my* department, you see. I'll fetch him round, if you'll wait here a minute; he'd like to hear what you think about the 'orse.

[*He goes off to the coachman's quarters.*

Undershell (alone). A very civil fellow this; he seems quite anxious to show me this animal! There must be *something* very remarkable about it.

[ADAMS *returns with* CHECKLEY.

Adams. Mr. Checkley, our 'ed coachman, Mr.

Undershell. He's coming in along with us to 'ear what you say, if you've no objections.

Undershell (*to himself*). I must make a friend of this coachman, or else—— (*Aloud.*) I shall be charmed, Mr. Checkley. I've only a very few minutes to spare; but I'm most curious to see this horse of yours.

Checkley. He ain't one o' *my* 'orses, sir. If he 'ad been—— But there, I'd better say nothing about it.

Adams (*as he leads the way into the stables, and turns up the gas*). There, sir, that's Deerfoot over there in the loose box.

Undershell (*to himself*). He seems to me much like any *other* horse! However, I can't be wrong in admiring. (*Aloud, as he inspects him through the rails.*) Ah, indeed? he *is* worth seeing! A magnificent creature!

Adams (*stripping off* Deerfoot's *clothing*). He's a good 'orse, sir. Her ladyship won't trust herself on no other animal, not since she 'ad the influenzy so bad. She'd take on dreadful if I 'ad to tell her he wouldn't be fit for no more work, she would!

Undershell (*sympathetically*). I can quite imagine so. Not that he seems in any danger of *that!*

Checkley (*triumphantly*). There, you 'ear that, Adams? The minute he set eyes on the 'orse:

Adams. Wait till Mr. Undershell has seen him move a bit, and see what he says *then*.

Checkley. If it was what *you* think, he'd never be standing like he is now, depend upon it.

Adams. You *can't* depend upon it. He 'eard us coming, and he's quite artful enough to draw his foot back for fear o' getting a knock. (*To* UNDERSHELL.) I've noticed him very fidgety-like on his forelegs this last day or two.

Undershell. Have you, though? (*To himself.*) I hope he won't be fidgety with his *hind*-legs. I shall stay outside.

Adams. I cooled him down with a rubub and aloes ball, and kep 'im on low diet; but he don't seem no better.

Undershell (*to himself*). I didn't gather the horse was unwell. (*Aloud.*) Dear me! no better? You don't say so!

Checkley. If you'd rubbed a little embrocation into the shoulder, you'd ha' done more good, in *my* opinion, and it's my belief as Mr. Undershell here will tell you I'm right.

Undershell (*to himself*). Can't afford to offend the coachman! (*Aloud.*) Well, I dare say—er—embrocation *would* have been better.

Adams. Ah, that's where me and Mr. Checkley

differ. According to me, it ain't to do with the shoulder at all—it's a deal lower down. . . . I'll 'ave him out of the box and you'll soon see what I mean.

Undershell (*hastily*). Pray don't trouble on my account. I—I can see him capitally from where I am, thanks.

Adams. You know best, sir. Only I thought you'd be better able to form a judgment after you'd seen the way he stepped across. But if you was to come in and examine the frog?— I don't like the look of it myself.

Undershell (*to himself*). I'm sure *I* don't. I've a horror of reptiles. (*Aloud.*) You're very good. I— I think I won't come in. The place must be rather damp, mustn't it—for that?

Adams. It's dry enough in 'ere, sir, as you may see; nor yet he ain't been standing about in no wet. Still, there it *is*, you see!

Undershell (*to himself*). What a fool he must be not to drive it out! Of course it must annoy the horse. (*Aloud*). I don't see it; but I'm quite willing to take your word for it.

Adams. I don't know how you can *expect* to see it, sir, without you look inside of the 'oof for it.

Undershell (*to himself*). It's not alive — it's

something *inside* the hoof. I suppose I ought to have known that. (*Aloud.*) Just so; but I see no necessity for looking inside the hoof.

Checkley. In course he don't, or he'd ha' looked the very fust thing, with all his experience. I 'ope you're satisfied *now*, Adams?

Adams. I can't say as I am. I say as no man can examine a 'orse thoroughly at that distance, be he who he may. And whether I'm right or wrong, it 'ud be more of a satisfaction to me if Mr. Undershell was to step in and see the 'oof for himself.

Checkley. Well, there's sense in that, and I dessay Mr. Undershell won't object to obliging you that far.

Undershell (with reluctance). Oh, with pleasure, if you make a point of it.

[*He enters the loose box delicately.*

Adams (picking up one of the horse's feet). Now, tell me how this 'ere 'oof strikes you.

Undershell (to himself). That hoof *can't;* but I'm not so sure about the others. (*Aloud, as he inspects it.*) Well—er—it seems to me a very *nice* hoof.

Adams (grimly). I was not arsking your opinion of it as a work of *art*, sir. Do you see any narrering coming on, or do you not? That's what I should like to get out of *you!*

Undershell (to himself). Does this man suppose

L

I *collect* hoofs! However, I'm not going to commit myself. (*Aloud.*) H'm—well, I—I rather agree with Mr. Checkley.

Checkley. I knew he would! Now you've *got* it, Adams! *I* can see Mr. Undershell knows what he's about.

Adams (*persistently*). But look at this 'ere pastern. You can't deny there's puffiness there. How do you get over *that?*

Undershell. If the horse is puffy, it's *his* business to get over it—not mine.

Adams (*aggrieved*). You may think proper to treat it light, sir; but if you put your 'and down 'ere, above the coronet, you'll feel a throbbing as plain as——

Undershell. Very likely. But I don't know, really, that it would afford me any particular gratification if I *did!*

Adams. Well, if you don't take *my* view, I should ha' thought as you'd want to feel the 'orse's pulse.

Undershell. You are quite mistaken. I don't. (*To himself.*) Particularly as I shouldn't know where to find it. What a bore this fellow is with his horse!

Checkley. In course, sir, *you* see what's running in Mr. Adams's 'ed all this time, what he's a-driving at, eh?

Undershell (to himself). I only wish I did! This will require tact. (*Aloud.*) I—I could hardly avoid seeing *that*—could I?

Checkley. I should think not. And it stands to reason as a vet like yourself 'd spot a thing like navickler fust go off.

Undershell (to himself). A vet! They've been taking me for a vet all this time! I can't have been so ignorant as I thought. I really don't like to undeceive them—they might feel annoyed. (*Aloud, knowingly.*) To be sure, I—I spotted it at once.

Adams. He *does* make it out navicular after all! What did I tell you, Checkley? Now p'raps you'll believe *me!*

Checkley. I'll be shot if that 'orse has navickler, whoever says so—there!

Adams (gloomily). It's the 'orse 'll 'ave to be shot; worse luck! I'd ha' give something if Mr. Undershell could ha' shown I was wrong; but there was very little doubt in *my* mind what it was all along.

Undershell (to himself, horrified). I've been pronouncing this unhappy animal's doom without knowing it! I must tone it down. (*Aloud.*) No—no, I never said he must be shot. There's no reason to despair. It—it's quite a mild form of er—clavicular —not at all infectious at present. And the horse

has a splendid constitution. I—I really think he'll
soon be himself again, if we only—er—leave Nature
to do her work, you know.

Adams (*after a prolonged whistle*). Well, if Nature
ain't better up in her work than you seem to be, it's
'igh time she chucked it, and took to something else.
You've a lot to learn about navicular, *you* 'ave, if
you can talk such rot as that!

Checkley. Ah, I've 'ad to do with a vet or two in
my time, but I'm blest if I ever come across the
likes o' *you* afore!

Undershell (*to himself*). I *knew* they'd find me out!
I must pacify them. (*Aloud.*) But, look here, I'm
not a vet. I never said I *was*. It was your mistake
entirely. The fact is, my—my good men, I came
down here because—well, it's unnecessary to explain
now *why* I came. But I'm most anxious to get
away, and if you, my dear Mr. Checkley, could let
me have a trap to take me to Shuntingbridge to-
night, I should feel extremely obliged.

[CHECKLEY *stares, deprived of speech.*

Adams (*with a private wink to* CHECKLEY). Certainly he will, sir. I'm sure Checkley 'll feel proud
to turn out, late as it is, to oblige a gentleman with
your remarkable knowledge of 'orseflesh. Drive you
over hisself in the broom and pair, *I* shouldn't wonder!

"YOU'VE A LOT TO LEARN ABOUT NAVICULAR, YOU 'AVE, IF YOU CAN TALK SUCH
ROT AS THAT!"

Undershell. *One* horse will be quite sufficient. Very well, then.   I'll just run up and get my portmanteau, and—and one or two things of mine, and if you will be round at the back entrance—don't trouble to drive up to the *front* door—as soon as possible, I won't keep you waiting longer than I can help.   Good evening, Mr. Adams, and many thanks. (*To himself, as he hurries back to the house.*)   I've got out of that rather well.   Now, I've only to find my way to the Verney Chamber, see this fellow Spurrell, and get my clothes back, and then I can retreat with comfort, and even dignity!   These Culverins shall learn that there is at least *one* poet who will not put up with their insolent patronage !

Checkley (*to* ADAMS).   He *has* got a cool cheek, and no mistake!   But if he waits to be druv over to Shuntingbridge till *I* come round for him, he'll 'ave to set on that portmanteau of his a goodish time!

Adams.   He did you pretty brown, I must say. To 'ear you crowing over me when he was on your side.   I could 'ardly keep from larfing !

Checkley.   I see he warn't no vet long afore you, but I let it go on for the joke of it.   It was rich to see you a-wanting him to feel the 'oof, and give it out navickler.   Well, you got his opinion for what it was wuth, so *you're* all right !

Adams. You think nobody knows anything about 'orses but yourself, you do; but if you're meanin' to make a story out o' this against me, why, I shall tell it *my* way, that's all!

Checkley. It was you he made a fool of, not me—and I can prove it—there!

> [*They dispute the point, with rising warmth, for some time.*

Adams (*calming down*). Well, see 'ere, Checkley, I dunno, come to think of it, as either on us 'll show up partickler smart over this 'ere job; and it strikes me we'd better both agree to keep quiet about it, eh? (CHECKLEY *acquiesces, not unwillingly.*) And I think I'll take a look in at the 'ousekeeper's-room presently, and try if I can't drop a hint to old Tredwell about that smooth-tongued chap, for it's my belief he ain't down 'ere for no good!

PART XV

TRAPPED!

In a Gallery outside the Verney Chamber.
TIME—*About* 10.15 P.M.

Undershell (*to himself, as he emerges from a back
staircase*). I suppose this *is* the corridor? The boy
said the name of the room was painted up over the
door. . . . Ah, there it is; and, yes, Mr. Spurrell's
name on a card. . . . The door is ajar; he is probably waiting for me inside. I shall meet him quite
temperately, treat it simply as a—— (*He enters;
a waste-paper basket, containing an ingenious arrangement of liquid and solid substances, descends on his
head.*) What the devil do you mean, sir, by this
outrageous——? All dark! Nobody here! Is
there a general conspiracy to insult me? Have I
been lured up here for a brutal—— (SPURRELL
bursts in.) Ah, *there* you are, sir! (*With cold*

dignity, through the lattice-work of the basket.) Will you kindly explain what this means ?

Spurrell. Wait till I strike a light. (*After lighting a pair of candles.*) Well, sir, if *you* don't know why you're ramping about like that under a waste-paper basket, I can hardly be expected to——

Undershell. I was determined not to remove it until somebody came in; it fell on my head the moment I entered; it contained something in a soap-dish, which has wetted my face. You may laugh, sir, but if this is a sample of your aristo-cratic——

Spurrell. If you could only see yourself ! But *I*'d nothing to do with it, 'pon my word I hadn't; only just this minute got away from the hall. . . . *I* know ! It's that sulky young beggar, Bearpark. I remember he slipped off on some excuse or other just now. He must have come in here and fixed that affair up for me—confound him !

Undershell. I think *I*'m the person most entitled to—— But no matter; it is merely one insult more among so many. I came here, sir, for a purpose, as you are aware.

Spurrell (*ruefully*). Your dress clothes ? All right, you shall have them directly. I wouldn't have put 'em on if I'd known they'd be wanted so soon.

Undershell. I should have thought your own would have been more comfortable.

Spurrell. More comfortable! I believe you. Why, I assure you I feel like a Bath bun in a baby's sock! But how was I to know? You shouldn't leave your things about like that!

Undershell. It is usual, sir, for people to come to a place like this provided with evening clothes of their own.

Spurrell. I know that as well as you do. Don't you suppose I'm unacquainted with the usages of society! Why, I've stayed in boarding-houses at the seaside many a time where it was *de rigger* to dress—even for high tea! But coming down, as I did, on business, it never entered my head that I should want my dress suit. So, when I found them all as chummy and friendly as possible, and expecting me to dine as a matter of course,—why, I can tell you I was too jolly glad to get hold of anything in the shape of a swallowtail and white choker to be over particular!

Undershell. You seem to have been more fortunate in your reception than I. But then *I* had not the advantage of being here in a business capacity.

Spurrell. Well, it wasn't that altogether. You see, I'm a kind of a celebrity in my way.

Undershell. I should hardly have thought *that* would be a recommendation here.

Spurrell. I was surprised myself to find what a lot they thought of it ; but, bless you, they're all as civil as shopwalkers ; and, as for the ladies, why, the old Countess and Lady Maisie and Lady Rhoda couldn't be more complimentary if I'd won the Victoria Cross, instead of getting a first prize for breeding and exhibiting a bull-bitch at Cruft's Dog show ! .

Undershell (*bitterly, to himself*). And this is our aristocracy ! They make a bosom friend of a breeder of dogs ; and find a poet only fit to associate with their servants ! What a theme for a satirist ! (*Aloud.*) I see nothing to wonder at. You possess precisely the social qualifications most likely to appeal to the leisured class.

Spurrell. Oh, there's a lot of humbug in it, mind you ! Most of 'em know about as much of the points of a bull as the points of a compass, only they let on to know a lot because they think it's smart. And some of 'em are after a pup from old Drummy's next litter. *I* see through all that, you know !

Undershell. You are a cynic, I observe, sir. But possibly the nature of the business which brings you here renders them——

Spurrell. That's the rummest thing about it. I haven't heard a word about that yet. I'm in the veterinary profession, you know. Well, they sent for me to see some blooming horse, and never even ask me to go near it! Seems odd, don't it?

Undershell (*to himself*). *I* had to go near the blooming horse! Now I begin to understand; the very servants did not expect to find a professional vet in any company but their own! (*Aloud.*) I—I trust that the horse will not suffer through any delay.

Spurrell. So do I; but how do I know that some ignorant duffer mayn't be treating him for the wrong thing? It may be all up with the animal before I get a chance of seeing what I can do?

Undershell (*to himself*). If he knew how near I went to getting the poor beast shot! But I needn't mention that now.

Spurrell. I don't say it isn't gratifying to be treated like a swell, but I've got my professional reputation to consider, you know; and if they're going to take up all my time talking about Andromeda——

Undershell (*with a start*). Andromeda! They have been talking about Andromeda? To you! Then it's *you* who——

Spurrell. Haven't I been telling you? I should

just jolly well think they *have* been talking about her! So you didn't know my bull's name was Andromeda before, eh? But *you* seem to have heard of her, too!

Undershell (*slowly*). I—I *have* heard of Andromeda—yes. [*He drops into a chair, dazed.*

Spurrell (*complacently*). It's curious how that bitch's fame seems to have spread. Why, even the old Bishop—— But, I say, you're looking rather queer; anything the matter with you, old fellow?

Undershell (*faintly*). Nothing — nothing. I — I feel a little giddy, that's all. I shall be better presently. [*He conceals his face.*

Spurrell (*in concern*). It was having that basket down on your head like that. Too bad! Here, I'll get you some water. (*He bustles about.*) I don't know if you're aware of it, old chap, but you're in a regular *dooce* of a mess!

Undershell (*motioning him away irritably*). Do you suppose I don't know *that*? For Heaven's sake, don't speak to me! let me alone! . . . I want to think—I want to think. (*To himself.*) I see it all now! I've made a hideous mistake! I thought these Culverins were deliberately—— And all the time—— Oh, what an unspeakable idiot I've been! . . . And I can't even explain! . . . The only thing to do is to escape before this fellow suspects the truth. It's lucky I ordered that carriage! (*Aloud, rising.*) I'm all right now; and—and I can't stay here any longer. I am leaving directly—directly!

Spurrell. You must give me time to get out of this toggery, old chap; you'll have to pick me out of it like a lobster!

Undershell (*wildly*). The clothes? Never mind them now. I can't wait. Keep them!

Spurrell. Do you really mean it, old fellow? If you *could* spare 'em a bit longer, I'd be no end obliged. Because, you see, I promised Lady Rhoda to come and finish a talk we were having, and they've taken away my own things to brush, so I haven't a rag to go down in except these; and they'd all think it so beastly rude if I went to bed now!

Undershell (*impatiently*). I tell you you may keep them, if you'll only go away!

Spurrell. But where am I to send the things to when I've done with 'em?

Undershell. What do I—— Stay, here's my card. Send them to that address. Now go and finish your evening!

Spurrell (*gratefully*). You *are* a rattling good chap, and no mistake! Though I'm hanged if I can quite make out what you're doing here, you know!

Undershell. It's not at all necessary that you *should* make it out. I am leaving immediately, and —and I don't wish Sir Rupert or Lady Culverin to hear of this—you understand?

Spurrell. Well, it's no business of mine; you've behaved devilish well to me, and I'm not surprised that you'd rather not be seen in the state you're in. I shouldn't like it myself!

Undershell. State? *What* state?

Spurrell. Ah, I *wondered* whether you knew. You'll see what I mean when you've had a look at yourself in the glass. I dare say it'll come off right enough. I can't stop. Ta, ta, old fellow, and thanks awfully! [*He goes out.*

Undershell (alone). What does he mean? But I've no time to waste. Where have they put my portmanteau? I can't give up *everything.* (*He hunts round the room, and eventually discovers a door leading into a small dressing-room.*) Ah, it's in there. I'll get it out, and put my things in. (*As he rushes back, he suddenly comes face to face with his own reflection in a cheval glass.*) Wh—who's that? Can this — this piebald horror possibly be — *me?* How——? Ah, it was *ink* in that infernal basket —not water! And my hair's full of flour! I *can't* go into a hotel like this, they'd think I was an

HE SUDDENLY COMES FACE TO FACE WITH HIS OWN REFLECTION.

escaped lunatic! (*He flies to a wash-hand stand, and scrubs and sluices desperately, after which he inspects the result in the mirror.*) It's not *nearly* off yet! Will *anything* get rid of this streakiness? (*He soaps and scrubs once more.*) And the flour's caked in my hair now! I must brush it all out before I am fit to be seen. (*He gradually, after infinite toil, succeeds in making himself slightly more presentable.*) Is the carriage waiting for me all this time? (*He pitches things into his portmanteau in a frantic flurry.*) What's that? Some one's coming!

[*He listens.*

Tredwell (outside). It's my conviction you've been telling me a pack o' lies, you young rascal. For what hearthly business that feller Undershell could 'ave in the Verney—— However, *I'll* soon see how it is. (*He knocks.*) Is any one in 'ere?

Undershell (to himself, distractedly). He mustn't find me here! Yet, where—— Ah, it's the only place!

[*He blows out the candles, and darts into the dressing-room as* TREDWELL *enters.*

Tredwell. The boy's right. He *is* in here; them candles is smouldering still. (*He relights one, and looks under the bed.*) You'd better come out o' that, Undershell, and give an account of yourself—

M

do you 'ear me? . . . He ain't under there! (*He
tries the dressing-room door;* UNDERSHELL *holds his
breath, and clings desperately to the handle.*) Very
well, sir, I know you're *there*, and I've no time to
trouble with you at present, so you may as well stay
where you are till you're wanted. I've 'eard o' your
goings-on from Mr. Adams, and I shall 'ave to fetch
Sir Rupert up to 'ave a talk with you by and bye.

[*He turns the key upon him, and goes.*
Undershell (*to himself, overwhelmed, as the butler's
step is heard retreating.*) And I came down here to
assert the dignity of Literature!

PART XVI

AN INTELLECTUAL PRIVILEGE

In the Chinese Drawing-room. TIME—*About*
9.45 P.M.

Mrs. Earwaker. Yes, dear Lady Lullington, I've always insisted on each of my girls adopting a distinct line of her own, and the result has been *most* satisfactory. Louisa, my eldest, is literary; she had a little story accepted not long ago by *The Milky Way;* then Maria is musical—practices regularly three hours every day on her violin. Fanny has become quite an expert in photography — kodaked her father the other day in the act of trying a difficult stroke at billiards; a back view—but *so* clever and characteristic!

Lady Lullington (absently). A back view? How *nice!*

Mrs. Earwaker. He was the only one of the family who didn't recognize it at once. Then my youngest

Caroline—well, I must say that for a long time I was quite in despair about Caroline. It really looked as if there was no single thing that she had the slightest bent or inclination for. So at last I thought she had better take up religion, and make *that* her speciality.

Lady Lullington (languidly). Religion! How *very* nice!

Mrs. Earwaker. Well, I got her a *Christian Year* and a covered basket, and quantities of tracts, and so on; but, somehow, she didn't seem to get *on* with it. So I let her give it up; and now she's gone in for poker-etching instead.

Lady Lullington (by an act of unconscious cerebration). Poker-etching! How very, *very* nice!
[*Her eyelids close gently.*

Lady Rhoda. Oh, but indeed, Lady Culverin, I thought he was perfectly charmin': not a bit booky, you know, but as clever as he can stick; knows more about terriers than any man I ever met!

Lady Culverin. So glad you found him agreeable, my dear. I was half afraid he might strike you as —well, just a little bit *common* in his way of talking.

Lady Rhoda. P'raps—but, after all, one can't expect those sort of people to talk quite like we do ourselves, *can* one?

Lady Cantire. Is that Mr. Spurrell you are finding

fault with, Albinia?   It is curious that *you* should be the one person here who—— I consider him a very worthy and talented young man, and I shall most certainly ask him to dinner—or *lunch*, at all events—as soon as we return. I dare say Lady Rhoda will not object to come and meet him.

Lady Rhoda. Rather not.   *I*'ll come, like a shot!

Lady Culverin (to herself). I suppose it's very silly of me to be so prejudiced. Nobody else seems to mind him!

Miss Spelwane (crossing over to them). Oh, Lady Culverin, Lady Lullington has such a *delightful* idea —she's just been saying how very, very nice it would be if Mr. Spurrell could be persuaded to read some of his poetry aloud to us presently. *Do* you think it could be managed ?

Lady Culverin (in distress). Really, my dear Vivien, I—I don't know *what* to say. I fancy people would so *much* rather talk—don't you think so, Rohesia?

Lady Cantire. Probably they would, Albinia.   It is most unlikely that they would care to hear any-thing more intellectual and instructive than the sound of their own voices.

Miss Spelwane. I *told* Lady Lullington that I was afraid you would think it a bore, Lady Cantire.

Lady Cantire. You are perfectly mistaken, Miss Spelwane. I flatter myself I am quite as capable of appreciating a literary privilege as anybody here. But I cannot answer for its being so acceptable to the majority.

Lady Culverin. No, it wouldn't do at all. And it would be making this young man so *much* too conspicuous.

Lady Cantire. You are talking nonsense, my dear. When you are fortunate enough to secure a celebrity at Wyvern, you can't make him *too* conspicuous. I never knew that Laura Lullington had any taste for literature before, but there's something to be said for her suggestion—if it can be carried out; it would at least provide a welcome relief from the usual after-dinner dullness of this sort of gathering.

Miss Spelwane. Then—would *you* ask him, Lady Cantire?

Lady Cantire. I, my dear? You forget that *I* am not hostess here. My sister-in-law is the proper person to do that.

Lady Culverin. Indeed I couldn't. But perhaps, Vivien, if you liked to suggest it to him, he might——

Miss Spelwane. I'll try, dear Lady Culverin. And if my poor little persuasions have no effect, I shall

fall back on Lady Cantire, and then he *can't* refuse.
I must go and tell dear Lady Lullington—she'll be
so pleased! (*To herself, as she skims away.*)   I
generally *do* get my own way.   But I mean him to
do it to please *Me!*

Lady Cantire (*to herself*). I must say that girl is
very much improved in manner since I last saw
anything of her.

Mrs. Chatteris (*a little later, to* Lady MAISIE).
Have you heard what a treat is in store for us?
That delightful Mr. Spurrell is going to give us a
reading or a recitation, or something, from his own
poems; at least Miss Spelwane is to ask him as
soon as the men come in.   Only *I* should have
thought that he would be much more likely to
consent if *you* asked him.

Lady Maisie. Would you?   I'm sure I don't know
why.

Mrs. Chatteris (*archly*). Oh, he took me in to
dinner, you know, and it's quite wonderful how
people confide in me, but I suppose they feel I can
be trusted.   He mentioned a little fact, which gave
me the impression that a certain fair lady's wishes
would be supreme with him.

Lady Maisie (*to herself*). The wretch!   He *has*
been boasting of my unfortunate letter!   (*Aloud.*)

Mr. Spurrell had no business to give you any impression of the kind. And the mere fact that I— that I happened to admire his verses——

Mrs. Chatteris. Exactly! Poets' heads are so easily turned; and, as I said to Captain Thick-nesse——

Lady Maisie. Captain Thicknesse! You have been talking about it—to *him!*

Mrs. Chatteris. I'd no idea you would mind any-body knowing, or I would never have dreamed of—— I've such a perfect *horror* of gossip! It took me so much by surprise, that I simply couldn't resist. But I can easily tell Captain Thicknesse it was all a mistake; *he* knows how fearfully inaccurate I always am.

Lady Maisie. I would rather you said nothing more about it, please; it is really not worth while contradicting anything so utterly absurd. (*To her-self.*) That Gerald—Captain Thicknesse—of all people, should know of my letter! And goodness only knows what story she may have made out of it!

Mrs. Chatteris (to herself, as she moves away). I've been letting my tongue run away with me, as usual. She's *not* the original of "Lady Grisoline," after all. Perhaps he meant Vivien Spelwane—the description was much more like *her!*

Pilliner (who has just entered with some of the younger men, to Miss SPELWANE). What *are* you doing with these chairs ? Why are we all to sit in a circle, like Moore and Burgess people ? You're *not* going to set the poor dear Bishop down to play baby-games ? How perfectly barbarous of you !

Miss Spelwane. The chairs are being arranged for something much more intellectual. We are going to get Mr. Spurrell to read a poem to us, if you want to know. I *told* you I should manage it.

Pilliner. There's only one drawback to that highly desirable arrangement. The songster has unostentatiously retired to roost. So I'm afraid you'll have to do without your poetry this evening—that is, unless you care to avail yourself again of *my* services ?

Miss Spelwane (indignantly). It is too *mean* of you. You must have told him !

[*He protests his innocence.*

Lady Rhoda. Archie, what's become of Mr. Spurrell ? I particularly want to ask him something.

Bearpark. The poet ? He nipped upstairs—as I told you all along he meant to—to scribble some of his democratic drivel, and (*with a suppressed grin*) I don't *think* you'll see him again this evening.

Captain Thicknesse (to himself, as he enters). She's keepin' a chair next hers in the corner there for somebody. Can it be for that poet chap? . . . (*He meets* Lady MAISIE'S *eye suddenly.*) Great Scott! If she means it for *me!* . . . I've half a mind not to—— No, I shall be a fool if I lose such a chance! (*He crosses, and drops into the vacant chair next hers.*) I *may* sit here, mayn't I?

Lady Maisie (*simply*). I meant you to. We used to be such good friends; it's a pity to have mis-understandings. And—and I want to ask you what that silly little Mrs. Chatteris has been telling you at dinner about me.

Captain Thicknesse. Well, she was sayin'—and I must say I don't understand it, after your tellin' me you knew nothing about this Mr. Spurrell till this afternoon——

Lady Maisie. But I don't. And I—I *did* offer to explain, but you said you weren't curious!

Captain Thicknesse. Didn't want you to tell me anything that perhaps you'd rather not, don't you know. Still, I *should* like to know how this poet chap came to write a poem all about you, and call it "Lady Grisoline," if he never——

Lady Maisie. But it's too ridiculous! How *could* he? When he never saw me, so far as I know, in all his life before!

Captain Thicknesse. He told Mrs. Chatteris you

were the original of his "Lady Grisoline" anyway,
and really——

Lady Maisie. He dared to tell her that? How
disgracefully impertinent of him. (*To herself.*) So
long as he hasn't talked about my letter, he may say
what he pleases!

Captain Thicknesse. But what *was* it you were goin'
to explain to me? You said there was somethin'——

Lady Maisie (*to herself*). It's no use; I'd sooner
die than tell him about that letter now! (*Aloud.*)
I—I only wished you to understand that, whatever
I think about poetry—I detest poets!

Lady Cantire. Yes, as you say, Bishop, a truly
Augustan mode of recreation. Still, Mr. Spurrell
doesn't seem to have come in yet, so I shall have
time to hear anything you have to say in defence of
your opposition to Parish Councils.

[*The* Bishop *resigns himself to the inevitable.*
Archie (*in* Pilliner's *ear*). Ink and flour—couldn't
possibly miss him; the bard's got a matted head *this*
time, and no mistake.

Pilliner. Beastly bad form, *I* call it—with a fellow
you don't know. You'll get yourself into trouble
some day. And you couldn't even bring your own
ridiculous booby-trap off, for here the beggar comes,
as if nothing had happened.

"INK AND FLOUR—COULDN'T POSSIBLY MISS HIM."

Archie (*disconcerted*). Confound him! The best booby trap I *ever* made!

The Bishop. My dear Lady Cantire, here *is* our youthful poet, at the eleventh hour. (*To himself.*) " *Sic me servavit* Apollo ! "

> [Miss SPELWANE *advances to meet* SPURRELL, *who stands surveying the array of chairs in blank bewilderment.*

PART XVII

A BOMB SHELL

In a Gallery near the Verney Chamber. TIME—*Same as that of the preceding Part.*

Spurrell (*to himself*). I must say it's rather rough luck on that poor devil. I get his dress suit, and all *he* comes in for is my booby-trap! (PHILLIPSON, *wearing a holland blouse over her evening toilette, approaches from the other end of the passage; he does not recognise her until the moment of collision.*) Emma!! It's never *you!* How do you come to be *here?*

Phillipson (*to herself*). Then it *was* my Jem after all! (*Aloud, distantly.*) I'm here in attendance on Lady Maisie Mull, being her maid. If I was at all curious—which I'm not—I might ask you what *you're* doing in such a house as this; and in evening dress, if you please!

Spurrell. I'm in evening dress, Emma, such as it is (not that I've any right to find fault with it); but

I'm in evening dress (*with dignity*) because I've been included in the dinner party here.

Phillipson. You must have been getting on since *I* knew you. Then you were studying to be a horse-doctor.

Spurrell. I *have* got on. I am now a qualified M.R.C.V.S.

Phillipson. And does that qualify you to dine with bishops and countesses and baronets and the gentry, like one of themselves?

Spurrell. I don't say it does, in itself. It was my Andromeda that did the trick, Emma.

Phillipson. Andromeda? They were talking of that downstairs. What made you take to scribbling, James?

Spurrell. Scribbling? how do you mean? My handwriting's easy enough to read, as you ought to know very well.

Phillipson. You can't expect me to remember what your writing's like; it's so long since I've seen it!

Spurrell. Come, I like that! When I wrote twice to say I was sorry we'd fallen out; and never got a word back!

Phillipson. If you'd written to the addresses I gave you abroad——

Spurrell. Then you *did* write; but none of the letters reached me. I never even knew you'd *gone* abroad. I wrote to the old place. And so did you, I suppose, not knowing I'd moved my lodgings too, so naturally—— But what does it all matter, so long as we've met and it's all right between us? Oh, my dear girl, if you only knew how I worried myself, thinking you were—— Well, all that's over now, isn't it? [*He attempts to embrace her.*

Phillipson (*repulsing him*). Not quite so fast, James. Before I say whether we're to be as we were or not, I want to know a little more about you. You wouldn't be here like this if you hadn't done *something* to distinguish yourself.

Spurrell. Well, I don't say I mayn't have got a certain amount of what they call "kudosh," owing to Andromeda. But what difference does that make?

Phillipson. Tell me, James, is it *you* that's been writing a pink book all over silver cutlets?

Spurrell. Me? Write a book—about cutlets—or anything else! Emma, you don't suppose I've quite come down to that! Andromeda's the name of my bull-dog. I took first prize with her; there were portraits of both of us in one of the papers. And the people here were very much taken with the dog, and—and so they asked me to dine with them That's how it was.

Phillipson. I should have thought, if they asked one of you to dine, it ought to have been the bull-dog.

Spurrell. **Now** what's the good of saying extravagant things of that sort? Not that old Drummy couldn't be trusted to behave anywhere!

Phillipson. Better than her master, I dare say. *I* heard of your goings on with some Lady Rhoda or other!

Spurrell. Oh, the girl I sat next to at dinner? Nice chatty sort of girl; seems fond of quadrupeds——

Phillipson. Especially two-legged ones! You see, I've been told all about it!

Spurrell. I assure you, I didn't go a step beyond the most ordinary civility. You're not going to be jealous because I promised I'd give her a liniment for one of her dogs, are you?

Phillipson. Liniment! You always *were* a flirt, James! But I'm not jealous. I've met a very nice-spoken young man while I've been here; he sat next to me at supper, and paid me the most beautiful compliments, and was most polite and attentive— though he hasn't got as far as liniment, at present.

Spurrell. But, Emma, you're not going to take up with some other fellow just when we've come together again?

Phillipson. If you call it "coming together," when I'm down in the housekeeper's room, and you're up above, carrying on with ladies of title!

N

Spurrell. Do you want to drive me frantic? As if I could help being where I am! How could I know *you* were here?

Phillipson. At all events, you know *now*, James. And it's for you to choose between your smart lady friends and me. If you're fit company for them, you're too grand for one of their maids.

Spurrell. My dear girl, don't be unreasonable! I'm expected back in the drawing-room, and I *can't* throw 'em over now all of a sudden without giving offence. There's the interests of the firm to consider, and it's not for me to take a lower place than I'm given. But it's only for a night or two, and you don't really suppose I wouldn't rather be where you are if I was free to choose—but I'm *not*, Emma, that's the worst of it!

Phillipson. Well, go back to the drawing-room, then; don't keep Lady Rhoda waiting for her liniment on my account. I ought to be in my ladies' rooms by this time. Only don't be surprised if, whenever you *are* free to choose, you find you've come back just too late—that's all!   [*She turns to leave him.*

Spurrell (detaining her). Emma, I won't let you go like this! Not before you've told me where I can meet you again here.

Phillipson. There's no place that I know of—

except the housekeeper's room; and of course you couldn't descend so low as that. . . . James, there's somebody coming! Let go my hand—do you want to lose me my character!

    [*Steps and voices are heard at the other end of*
          the passage; she frees herself, and escapes.

Spurrell (*attempting to follow*). But, Emma, stop one—— She's gone! . . . Confound it, there's the butler and a page-boy coming! It's no use staying up here any longer. (*To himself, as he goes downstairs.*) It's downright *torture*—that's what it is! To be tied by the leg in the drawing-room, doing the civil to a lot of girls I don't care a blow about; and to know that all the time some blarneying beggar downstairs is doing his best to rob me of my Emma! Flesh and blood can't stand it; and yet I'm blest if I see any way out of it without offending 'em all round.   [*He enters the Chinese Drawing-room.*

In the Chinese Drawing-room.

Miss Spelwane. At last, Mr. Spurrell! We began to think you meant to keep away altogether. Has anybody told you *why* you've been waited for so impatiently?

Spurrell (*looking round the circle of chairs apprehensively*). No. Is it family prayers, or what? Er —are they over?

Miss Spelwane. No, no; nothing of that sort. Can't you *guess?* Mr. Spurrell, I'm going to be very bold, and ask a great, *great* favour of you. I don't know why they chose *me* to represent them; I told Lady Lullington I was afraid my entreaties would have no weight; but if you only would——

Spurrell (to himself). They're at it again! How many *more* of 'em want a pup! (*Aloud.*) Sorry to be disobliging, but——

Miss Spelwane (joining her hands in supplication). Not if I *implore* you? Oh, Mr. Spurrell, I've quite set my heart on hearing you read aloud to us. Are you really cruel enough to refuse?

Spurrell. Read aloud! Is *that* what you want me to do? But I'm no particular hand at it. I don't know that I've ever read aloud—except a bit out of the paper now and then—since I was a boy at school!

Lady Cantire. What's that I hear? Mr. Spurrell professing incapacity to read aloud? Sheer affectation! Come, Mr. Spurrell, I am much mistaken if you are wanting in the power to thrill all hearts here. Think of us as instruments ready to respond to your touch. Play upon us as you will; but don't be so ungracious as to raise any further obstacles.

Spurrell (resignedly). Oh, very well, if I'm required to read, *I'm* agreeable. [*Murmurs of satisfaction.*

Lady Cantire. Hush, please, everybody! Mr.

Spurrell is going to read. My dear Bishop, if you *wouldn't* mind just—— Lord Lullington, can you hear where you are? Where are you going to sit, Mr. Spurrell? In the centre will be best. Will somebody move that lamp a little, so as to give him more light?

Spurrell (to himself, as he sits down). I wonder what we're supposed to be playing at! (*Aloud.*) Well, what am I to read, eh?

Miss Spelwane (placing an open copy of "Andromeda" *in his hands with a charming air of deferential dictation).* You might begin with *this*—such a *dear* little piece! I'm dying to hear *you* read it!

Spurrell (as he takes the book). I'll do the best I can! (*He looks at the page in dismay.*) Why, look here, it's *poetry!* I didn't bargain for that. Poetry's altogether out of my line! (*Miss* SPELWANE *opens her eyes to their fullest extent, and retires a few paces from him; he begins to read in a perfunctory monotone, with deepening bewilderment and disgust—*

"THE SICK KNIGHT.

Reach me the helmet from yonder rack,
  Mistress o' mine! with its plume of white:
Now help me upon my destrier's back,
  Mistress o' mine! though he swerve in fright.
And guide my foot to the stirrup-ledge,
  Mistress o' mine! it eludes me still.
Then fill me a cup as a farewell pledge,
  Mistress o' mine! for the night air's chill!

"YOU MIGHT BEGIN WITH THIS—SUCH A DEAR LITTLE PIECE."

Haste! with the buckler and pennon'd lance,
    Mistress o' mine! or ever I feel
My war-horse plunge in impatient prance,
    Mistress o' mine! at the prick of heel.
Pay scant heed to my pallid hue,
    Mistress o' mine! for the wan moon's sheen
Doth blazon the gules o' my cheek with blue,
    Mistress o' mine! or glamour it green.
One last long kiss, ere I seek the fray . . .
    Mistress o' mine! though I quit my sell,
I would meet the foe i' the mad mêlée.
    Mistress o' mine! an' I were but well!"

(*After the murmur of conventional appreciation has died away.*) Well, of course, I don't set up for a judge of such things myself, but I must say, if I was asked *my* opinion—of all the downright tommy-rot I *ever*—— (*The company look at one another with raised eyebrows and dropped underlips; he turns over the leaves backwards until he arrives at the title-page.*) I *say*, though, I do call this *rather* rum! Who the dickens is Clarion Blair? Because *I* never heard of him—and yet it seems he's been writing poetry on my bull-dog!

Miss Spelwane (*faintly*). Writing poetry—about your bull-dog!

Spurrell. Yes, the one you've all been praising up so. If it isn't meant for her, it's what you might call a most surprising coincidence, for here's the old dog's name as plain as it can be—*Andromeda!* [*Tableau.*

PART XVIII

THE LAST STRAW

After SPURRELL'S *ingenuous comments upon the volume in his hand, a painful silence ensues, which no one has sufficient presence of mind to break for several seconds.*

Miss Spelwane (to herself). Not Clarion Blair! Not even a poet! I—I could *slap* him!

Pilliner (to himself). Poor dear Vivien! But if people will insist on patting a strange poet, they mustn't be surprised if they get a nasty bite!

Lady Maisie (to herself). He *didn't* write *Andromeda!* Then he hasn't got my letter after all! And I've been such a *brute* to the poor dear man! *How* lucky I said nothing about it to Gerald!

Captain Thicknesse (to himself). So he *ain't* the bard! . . . Now I see why Maisie's been behavin' so oddly all the evenin'; she spotted him, and didn't like to speak out. Tried to give me a hint, though. Well, I shall stay out my leave now!

Lady Rhoda (to herself). I thought all along he seemed too good a sort for a poet!

Archie (to himself). It's all very well; but how about that skit he went up to write on us? He *must* be a poet of sorts.

Mrs. Brooke-Chatteris (to herself). This is fearfully puzzling. What made him say that about "Lady Grisoline"?

The Bishop (to himself). A crushing blow for the Countess; but not unsalutary. I am distinctly conscious of feeling more kindly disposed to that young man. Now why?   [*He ponders.*

Lady Lullington (to herself). I thought this young man was going to read us some more of his poetry; it's too tiresome of him to stop to tell us about his bull-dog. As if anybody cared *what* he called it!

Lord Lullington (to himself). Uncommonly awkward, this! If I could catch Laura's eye—but I suppose it would hardly be decent to go just yet.

Lady Culverin (to herself). Can Rohesia have known this? What possible object could she have had in—— And oh, dear, *how* disgusted Rupert will be!

Sir Rupert (to himself). Seems a decent young

chap enough! Too bad of Rohesia to let him in for
this.   I don't care a straw what he is—he's none
the worse for not being a poet.

Lady Cantire (to herself). What *is* he maundering
about?   It's utterly inconceivable that *I* should
have made any mistake.   It's only too clear what
the cause is—*Claret!*

Spurrell (aloud, good-humouredly).   Too bad of
you to try and spoof me like this before everybody,
Miss Spelwane! I don't know whose idea it was
to play me such a trick, but——

Miss Spelwane (indistinctly). Please understand
that nobody here had the *least* intention of playing
a trick upon you!

Spurrell. Well, if you say so, of course—— But
it looked rather like it, asking me to read when
I've about as much poetry in me as—as a pot hat!
Still, if I'm *wanted* to read aloud, I shall be happy
to——

Lady Culverin (hastily). Indeed, *indeed*, Mr. Spurrell, we couldn't think of troubling you any more
under the circumstances!   (*In desperation.*) Vivien,
my dear, won't you *sing* something?

> [*The company echo the request with unusual
>   eagerness.*

Spurrell (to himself, during Miss SPELWANE'S *song)*.

Wonder what's put them off being read to all of a sudden? My elocution mayn't be first-class, exactly, but still—— (*As his eye happens to rest on the binding of the volume on his knee.*) Hullo! This cover's pink, with silver things, not unlike cutlets, on it! Didn't Emma ask me——? By George, if it's *that!* I may get down to the housekeeper's room, after all! As soon as ever this squalling stops I'll find out; I *can't* go on like this! (Miss SPELWANE *leaves the piano; everybody plunges feverishly into conversation on the first subject—other than poetry or dogs—that presents itself, until* Lord *and* Lady LULLINGTON *set a welcome example of departure.*) Better wait till these county nobs have cleared, I suppose—there goes the last of 'em—now for it! . . . (*He pulls himself together, and approaches his host and hostess.*) Hem, Sir Rupert, and your ladyship, it's occurred to me that it's just barely possible you may have got it in your heads that I was something in the *poetical* way.

Sir Rupert (*to himself*). Not this poor young chap's fault; must let him down as easily as possible! (*Aloud.*) Not at all—not at all! Ha—assure you we quite understand; no necessity to say another word about it.

Spurrell (*to himself*). Just my luck! They quite

understand! No housekeeper's room for me this
journey! (*Aloud.*) Of course I knew the Countess,
there, and Lady Maisie, were fully aware all
along—— (*To* Lady MAISIE, *as stifled exclamations
reach his ear.*) You *were*, weren't you?

Lady Maisie (*hastily*). Yes, yes, Mr. Spurrell. Of
course! It's all *perfectly* right!

Spurrell (*to the others*). You see, I should never
have thought of coming in as a visitor if it hadn't
been for the Countess; she would *have* it that it
was all right, and that I needn't be afraid I shouldn't
be welcome.

Lady Culverin. To be sure—any friend of my
sister-in-law's——

Lady Cantire. Albinia, I have refrained from
speech as long as possible; but this is really *too*
much! You *don't* suppose I should have introduced
Mr. Spurrell here unless I had had the strongest
reasons for knowing, however he may be pleased
to mystify us now, that he, and nobody else, is the
author of *Andromeda!* And I, for one, absolutely
decline to believe in this preposterous story of his
about a bull-dog.

Spurrell. But your ladyship must have known!
Why, you as good as asked me on the way here
to put you down for a bull-pup!

Lady Cantire. Never, never! A bull-pup is the last creature I should ever dream of coveting. You were obliging enough to ask me to accept a presentation copy of your verses.

Spurrell. Was I? I don't exactly see how I *could* have been, considering I never made a rhyme in my life!

Sir Rupert. There, there, Rohesia, it was *your* mistake; but as we are indebted to it for the pleasure of making Mr. Spurrell's acquaintance——

Lady Cantire. I am not in the habit of making mistakes, Rupert. I don't know what you and Albinia and Maisie may know that I am in ignorance of, but, since you seem to have been aware from the first that Mr. Spurrell was not the poet you had invited here to meet me, will you kindly explain what has become of the *real* author?

Sir Rupert. My dear Rohesia, I don't know and I don't *care!*

Lady Cantire. There you are *wrong*, Rupert, because it's obvious that if he is not Mr. Spurrell, the real poet's absence has to be accounted for in *some* way.

Spurrell. By Jove, I believe I can put you on the track. I shouldn't wonder if he's the party these dress clothes of mine belong to! I dare say you may have noticed they don't look as if they were made for me ?

Lady Cantire (closing her eyes). Pray let us avoid any sartorial questions! We are waiting to hear about this person.

Spurrell. Well, I found I'd got on his things by mistake, and I went up as soon as I could after dessert to my room to take 'em off, and there he was, with a waste-paper basket on his head——

Lady Cantire. A waste-paper basket on his head! And pray what should he have *that* for ?

Spurrell. I'm no wiser than your ladyship *there.* All *I* know is he said he wouldn't take it off till he saw me. And I never saw any one in such a mess with ink and flour as he was !

Lady Cantire. Ink and flour, indeed! This rigmarole gets more ridiculous every moment! You can't seriously expect any one here to believe it !

[ARCHIE *discreetly retires to the smoking-room.*

Spurrell. Well, I rather think somebody must have fixed up a booby-trap for *me*, you know, and he happened to go in first and get the benefit of it. And he was riled, very naturally, thinking *I'd* done it, but after we'd had a little talk together, he calmed down and said I might keep his clothes, which I thought uncommonly good-natured of him, you know.

By the way, he gave me his card. Here it is, if your ladyship would like to see it.

[*He hands it to* Lady CULVERIN.

Lady Culverin. "Mr. Undershell!" . . . Rohesia, that *is* Clarion Blair! I *knew* it was *something* ending in "ell." (*To* SPURRELL.) And you say Mr. Undershell is here—in this house?

Spurrell. Not now. He's gone by this time.

The Others (*in dismay*). Gone!

Spurrell. He said he was leaving at once. If he'd only told me how it was, I'd have——

Lady Cantire. I don't believe a single word of all this! If Mr. Spurrell is not Clarion Blair, let him explain how he came to be coming down to Wyvern this afternoon!

Spurrell. If your ladyship doesn't really know, you had better ask Sir Rupert; *he'll* tell you it's all right.

Lady Cantire. Then perhaps *you* will be good enough to enlighten us, Rupert?

Sir Rupert (*driven into a corner*). Why, 'pon my word, I'm bound to say that I'm just as much in the dark as anybody else, if it comes to that!

Spurrell (*eagerly*). But you wired me to come, sir! About a horse of yours! I've been wondering all the evening when you'd tell me I could go round

"ALBINIA, I THINK I WILL GO TO BED."

and have a look at him. I'm here instead of Mr.
Spavin—*now* do you understand, Sir Rupert? I'm
the vet. [*Suppressed sensation.*

Sir Rupert (to himself). This is devilish awkward!
Don't quite know what to do. (*Aloud.*) To—to be
sure you are! Of course! That's it, Rohesia! Mr.
Spurrell came down to see a horse, and we shall be
very glad to have the benefit of his opinion by and
bye. [*He claps him amicably on the shoulder.*

Lady Cantire (in a sepulchral tone). Albinia, I
think I will go to bed. [*She withdraws.*

Sir Rupert (to himself). There'll be no harm in
letting him stay, now he *is* here. If Rohesia objects,
she's got nobody but herself to blame for it!

Spurrell (to himself). They won't want to keep me
upstairs much longer after this! (TREDWELL *enters,
and seems to have something of importance to com-
municate to* Sir RUPERT *in private.*) I wonder what
the dooce is up *now!*

[*Partial reaction in company.*

PART XIX

UNEARNED INCREMENT

Sir Rupert (*to* TREDWELL). Well, what is it ?

Tredwell (*in an undertone*). With reference to
the party, Sir Rupert, as represents himself to have
come down to see the 'orse, I——

Sir Rupert (*aloud*). You mean Mr. Spurrell ? It's
all right. Mr. Spurrell will see the horse to-morrow.
(TREDWELL *disguises his utter bewilderment.*) By the
way, we expected a Mr. —— What did you say
the name was, my dear ? . . . Undershell ? To be
sure, a Mr. Undershell, to have been here in time
for dinner. Do you know why he has been unable
to come before this ?

Tredwell (*to himself*). Do I know ? Oh, Lor !
(*Aloud.*) I—I believe he *have* arrived, Sir Rupert.

Sir Rupert. So I understand from Mr. Spurrell.
Is he here still ?

Tredwell. He is, Sir Rupert. I—I considered it
my dooty not to allow him to leave the house, not
feeling——

Sir Rupert. Quite right, Tredwell. I should have been most seriously annoyed if I had found that a guest we were all anxiously expecting had left the Court, owing to some fancied—— Where is he now?

Tredwell (faintly). In—in the Verney Chamber. Leastways——

Sir Rupert. Ah. (*He glances at* SPURRELL.) Then where——? But that can be arranged. Go up and explain to Mr. Undershell that we have only this moment heard of his arrival; say we understand that he has been obliged to come by a later train, and that we shall be delighted to see him, just as he is.

Spurrell (to himself). He was worth looking at just as he *was*, when *I* saw him!

Pilliner (to himself). By a later train? Then, how the deuce did his clothes——? Oh, well, however it was, it don't concern *me*.

Tredwell. Very good, Sir Rupert. (*To himself, as he departs.*) If I'm not precious careful over this job, it may cost me my situation!

Spurrell. Sir Rupert, I've been thinking that, after what's occurred, it would probably be more satisfactory to all parties if I shifted my quarters, and—took my meals in the housekeeper's room.

[Lady MAISIE *and* Lady RHODA *utter inarticulate protests.*

Sir Rupert. My *dear* sir, not on any account— couldn't *hear* of it! My wife, I'm sure, will say the same.

Lady Culverin (with an effort). I hope Mr. Spurrell will continue to be our guest precisely as before—that is, if he will forgive us for putting him into another room.

Spurrell (to himself). It's no use; I *can't* get rid of 'em; they stick to me like a lot of blooming burrs! (*Aloud, in despair.*) Your ladyship is very good, but—— Well, the fact is, I've only just found out that a young lady I've long been deeply attached to is in this very house. She's a Miss Emma Phillipson—maid, so I understand, to Lady Maisie—and, without for one moment wishing to draw any comparisons, or to seem ungrateful for all the friendliness I've received, I really and truly would feel myself more comfortable in a circle where I could enjoy rather more of my Emma's society than I can here!

Sir Rupert (immensely relieved). Perfectly natural! and—hum—sorry as we are to lose you, Mr. Spurrell, we—ah—mustn't be inconsiderate enough to keep you here a moment longer. I've no doubt you will find the young lady in the housekeeper's room —any one will tell you where it is. . . . Good night to you, then; and, remember, we shall expect to see you in the field on Tuesday.

"I'M SO VERY GLAD—ABOUT EMMA, YOU KNOW."

Lady Maisie. Good night, Mr. Spurrell, and—and I'm so very glad—about Emma, you know. I hope you will both be very happy.

[*She shakes hands warmly.*

Lady Rhoda. So do I. And mind you don't forget about that liniment, you know.

Captain Thicknesse (*to himself*). Maisie don't care a hang! And I was ass enough to fancy—— But there, that's all over now!

In the Verney Chamber.

Undershell (*in the dressing-room, to himself*). I wonder how long I've been locked up here—it seems hours! I almost hope they've forgotten me altogether. . . . Some one has come in. . . . If it should be Sir Rupert!! Great heavens, what a situation to be found in by one's host! . . . Perhaps it's only that fellow Spurrell; if so, there's a chance. (*The door is unlocked by* TREDWELL, *who has lighted the candles on the dressing table.*) It's the butler again. Well, I shall soon know the worst! (*He steps out, blinking, with as much dignity as possible.*) Perhaps you will kindly inform me why I have been subjected to this indignity?

Tredwell (*in perturbation*). I think, Mr. Undershell, sir, in common fairness, you'll admit as you've mainly yourself to thank for any mistakes that have occurred ; for which I 'asten to express my pussonal regret.

Undershell. So long as you realise that you have made a mistake, I am willing to overlook it, on condition that you help me to get away from this place without your master and mistress's knowledge.

Tredwell. It's too late, sir. They know you're 'ere !

Undershell. They know ! Then there's no time to be lost. I must leave this moment !

Tredwell. No, sir, excuse me ; but you can't hardly do that *now*. I was to say that Sir Rupert and the ladies would be glad to see you in the droring-room himmediate.

Undershell. Man alive ! do you imagine anything would induce me to meet them now, after the humiliations I have been compelled to suffer under this roof ?

Tredwell. If you would prefer anything that has taken place in the room, sir, or in the stables to be 'ushed up——

Undershell. Prefer it ! If it were only possible ! But they know—they *know !* What's the use of talking like that ?

Tredwell (to himself). I know where I am now ! (*Aloud.*) They know nothink up to the present, Mr. Undershell, nor yet I see no occasion why they should—leastwise from any of *Us*.

Undershell. But they know I'm here; how am I to account for all the time—— ?

Tredwell. Excuse me, sir. I thought of that, and it occurred to me as it might be more agreeable to your feelings, sir, if I conveyed an impression that you had only just arrived—'aving missed your train, sir.

Undershell (*overjoyed*). How am I to thank you? that was really most discreet of you—most considerate!

Tredwell. I am truly rejoiced to hear you say so, sir. And I'll take care nothing leaks out. And if you'll be kind enough to follow me to the droring-room, the ladies are waiting to see you.

Undershell (*to himself*). I may actually meet Lady Maisie Mull after all! (*Aloud, recollecting his condition.*) But I can't go down like this. I'm in such a horrible mess!

Tredwell. I reelly don't perceive it, sir; except a little white on your coat-collar behind. Allow me— there it's off now. (*He gives him a hand-glass*) If you'd like to see for yourself.

Undershell (*to himself as he looks*). A slight pallor, that's all. I am more presentable than I could have hoped. (*Aloud.*) Have the kindness to take me to Lady Culverin at once.

In the Chinese Drawing-room.　A few minutes later.

Sir Rupert (*to* UNDERSHELL, *after the introductions have been gone through*). And so you missed the 4.55 and had to come on by the 7.30 which stops everywhere, eh ?

Undershell. It—it certainly does stop at most stations.

Sir Rupert. And how did you get on to Wyvern—been here long ?

Undershell. N—not *particularly* long.

Sir Rupert. Fact is, you see, we made a mistake. Very ridiculous, but we've been taking that young fellow, Mr. Spurrell, for *you* all this time ; so we never thought of inquiring whether you'd come or not.　It was only just now he told us how he'd met you in the Verney Chamber, and the very handsome way, if you will allow me to say so, in which you had tried to efface yourself.

Undershell (*to himself*). I didn't expect him to take *that* view of it !　(*Aloud.*)　I—I felt I had no alternative.　[Lady MAISIE *regards him with admiration.*

Sir Rupert. You did an uncommon fine thing, sir, and I'm afraid you received treatment on your arrival which you had every right to resent.

Undershell (*to himself*). I hoped he didn't know about the housekeeper's room !　(*Aloud.*)　Please

say no more about it, Sir Rupert. I know now that
you were entirely innocent of any——

Sir Rupert (*horrified*). Good Gad! you didn't
suppose *I* had any hand in fixing up that booby-
trap, or whatever it was, did you? Young fellows
will get bear-fighting and playing idiotic tricks on
one another, and you seem to have been the victim—
that's how it was. Have you had anything to eat
since you came? If not——

Undershell (*hastily*). Thank you, I—I *have* dined.
(*To himself.*) So he *doesn't* know where, after all!
I will spare him *that*.

Sir Rupert. Got some food at Shuntingbridge, eh?
Afraid they gave you a wretched dinner?

Undershell. Quite the reverse, I assure you. (*To
himself.*) Considering that it came from his own table!

Pilliner (*to himself*). I *still* don't understand how
his clothes—— (*Aloud.*) Did you send your portmanteau on ahead, then, or what?

Undershell (*blankly*). Send my port—? I don't
understand.

Pilliner. Oh, I only asked, because the other man
said he was wearing your things.

Sir Rupert (*as* UNDERSHELL *remains speechless*). I
see how it was—perfectly simple—rush for the train
—porter put your luggage in—you got left behind,
wasn't that it?

Undershell. I—I certainly *did* get separated from my portmanteau, somehow, and I suppose it must have arrived before me. (*To himself.*) Considering the pace of the fly-horse, I think I am justified in assuming *that!*

Pilliner (*to himself*). Ass I was not to hold my tongue!

Lady Maisie (*in an undertone, to* Captain THICK-NESSE). Gerald, you remember what I said some time ago—about poetry and poets?

Captain Thicknesse. Perfectly. And I thought you were quite right.

Lady Maisie. I was quite *wrong*. I didn't know what I was talking about. I do now. Good night. (*She crosses to* UNDERSHELL.) Good night, Mr. Blair, I'm so very glad we have met—at last! [*She goes.*

Undershell (*to himself, rapturously*). She's *not* freckled; she's not even sandy. She's lovely! And, by some unhoped-for good fortune, all this has only raised me in her eyes. I am more than compensated!

Captain Thicknesse (*to himself*). I may just as well get back to Aldershot to-morrow—*now*. I'll go and prepare Lady C.'s mind, in case. It's hard luck; just when everything seemed goin' right! I'd give somethin' to have the other bard back, I know. It's no earthly use my tryin' to stand against *this* one!

PART XX

DIFFERENT PERSONS HAVE DIFFERENT OPINIONS

LADY MAISIE'S *Room at Wyvern.* TIME—*Saturday
night, about* 11.30.

Lady Maisie (*to* PHILLIPSON, *who is brushing her hair*).
You are *sure* mamma isn't expecting me? (*Irresolutely.*)
Perhaps I had better just run in and say good night.

Phillipson. I wouldn't recommend it, really, my
lady ; her ladyship seems a little upset in her nerves
this evening.

Lady Maisie (*to herself*). *Il-y-a de quoi!* (*Aloud, relieved.*) It might only disturb her, certainly.... I hope
they are making you comfortable here, Phillipson ?

Phillipson. Very much so indeed, thank you, my
lady. The tone of the room downstairs is *most* superior.

Lady Maisie. That's satisfactory. And I hear
you have met an old admirer of yours here—Mr.
Spurrell, I mean.

Phillipson. We *did* happen to encounter each other
in one of the galleries, my lady, just for a minute ;
though I shouldn't have expected *him* to allude to it !

Lady Maisie. Indeed! And why not?

Phillipson. Mr. James Spurrell appears to have elevated himself to a very different sphere from what he occupied when *I* used to know him, my lady; though how and why he comes to be where he is, I don't rightly understand myself at present.

Lady Maisie (to herself). And no wonder! I feel horribly guilty! (*Aloud.*) You mustn't blame poor Mr. Spurrell, Phillipson; *he* couldn't help it!

Phillipson (with studied indifference). I'm not blaming him, my lady. If he prefers the society of his superiors to mine, he's very welcome to do so; there's others only too willing to take his place!

Lady Maisie. Surely none who would be as fond of you or make so good a husband, Phillipson!

Phillipson. That's as maybe, my lady. There was one young man that travelled down in the same compartment, and sat next me at supper in the room. I could see he took a great fancy to me from the first, and his attentions were really quite pointed. I am sure I couldn't bring myself to repeat his remarks, they were so flattering!

Lady Maisie. Don't you think you will be rather a foolish girl if you allow a few idle compliments from a stranger to outweigh such an attachment as Mr. Spurrell seems to have for you?

Phillipson. If *he*'s found new friends, my lady, I consider myself free to act similarly.

Lady Maisie. Then you don't know? He told us quite frankly this evening that he had only just discovered you were here, and would much prefer to be where you were. He went down to the house-keeper's room on purpose.

Phillipson (*moved*). It's the first I've heard of it, my lady. It must have been after I came up. If I'd only known he'd behave like *that!*

Lady Maisie (*instructively*). You see how loyal he is to *you.* And now, I suppose, he will find he has been supplanted by this new acquaintance—some smooth-tongued, good-for-nothing valet, I dare say?

Phillipson (*injured*). Oh, my lady, indeed he wasn't a *man!* But there was nothing serious between us —at least, on *my* side—though he certainly did go on in a very sentimental way himself. However, he's left the Court by now, that's *one* comfort! (*To herself.*) I wish now I'd said nothing about him to Jem. If he was to get asking questions down-stairs—— He always *was* given to jealousy—reason or none!   [*A tap is heard at the door.*

Lady Rhoda (*outside*). Maisie, may I come in? if you've done your hair, and sent away your maid. (*She enters.*) Ah, I see you haven't.

Lady Maisie. Don't run away, Rhoda; my maid has just done. You can go now, Phillipson.

Lady Rhoda (to herself, as she sits down). Phillipson! So *that's* the young woman that funny vet man prefers to *us!* H'm, can't say I feel flattered!

Phillipson (to herself, as she leaves the room). This must be the Lady Rhoda, who was making up to my Jem! He wouldn't have anything to say to her, though; and, now I see her, I am not surprised at it!

[*She goes. A pause.*

Lady Rhoda (crossing her feet on the fender). Well, we can't complain of havin' had a dull evenin', *can* we?

Lady Maisie (taking a hand-screen from the mantel-shelf). Not altogether. Has—anything fresh happened since I left?

Lady Rhoda. Nothing particular. Archie apologised to this new man in the billiard-room. For the booby trap. We all told him he'd *got* to. And Mr. Carrion Bear, or Blundershell, or whatever he calls himself—*you* know—was so awf'lly gracious and condescendin' that I really thought poor dear old Archie would have wound up his apology by punchin' his head for him. Strikes me, Maisie, that mop-headed minstrel boy is a decided change for the worse. Doesn't it you?

Lady Maisie (toying with the screen). How do you mean, Rhoda?

"WELL, WE CAN'T COMPLAIN OF HAVIN' HAD A DULL EVENIN', CAN WE?"

Lady Rhoda. I meantersay I call Mr. Spurrell——
Well, he's real, anyway—he's a *man,* don't you know.
As for the other, so *feeble* of him missin' his train
like he did, and turnin' up too late for everything!
Now, *wasn't* it?

Lady Maisie. Poets *are* dreamy and unpractical
and unpunctual—it's their nature.

Lady Rhoda. Then they should stay at home.
Just see what a hopeless muddle he's got us all into!
I declare I feel as if anybody might turn into somebody else on the smallest provocation after this. I
know poor Vivien Spelwane will be worryin' her
pillows like rats most of the night, and I rather
fancy it will be a close time for poets with your
dear mother, Maisie, for some time to come. All
this silly little man's fault!

Lady Maisie. No, Rhoda. Not his—*ours.* Mine
and mamma's. We ought to have felt from the first
that there *must* be some mistake, that poor Mr.
Spurrell couldn't *possibly* be a poet! I don't know,
though—people generally *are* unlike what you'd expect from their books. I believe they do it on purpose!
Not that that applies to Mr. Blair; he *is* one's idea
of what a poet should be. If he hadn't arrived when
he did, I don't think I could ever have borne to read
another line of poetry as long as I lived!

P

Lady Rhoda. I *say!* Do you call him as good-lookin' as all *that?*

Lady Maisie. I was not thinking about his looks, Rhoda—it's his *conduct* that's so splendid.

Lady Rhoda. His conduct? Don't see anything splendid in missin' a train. I could do it myself if I tried?

Lady Maisie. Well, I wish I could think there were many men capable of acting so nobly and generously as he did.

Lady Rhoda. As how?

Lady Maisie. You really don't see! Well, then, you shall. He arrives late, and finds that somebody else is here already in his character. He makes no fuss; manages to get a private interview with the person who is passing as himself; when, of course, he soon discovers that poor Mr. Spurrell is as much deceived as anybody else. What is he to do? Humiliate the unfortunate man by letting him know the truth? Mortify my uncle and aunt by a public explanation before a whole dinner-party? That is what a stupid or a selfish man might have done, almost without thinking. But not Mr. Blair. He has too much tact, too much imagination, too much chivalry for that. He saw at once that his only course was to spare his host and hostess, and—and all of us a scene, by slipping away quietly and unostentatiously, as he had come.

Lady Rhoda (yawning). If he saw all that, why didn't he *do* it?

Lady Maisie (indignantly). Why? How provoking you can be, Rhoda! *Why?* Because that stupid Tredwell wouldn't let him! Because Archie delayed him by some idiotic practical joke! Because Mr. Spurrell went and blurted it all out! . . . Oh, don't try to run down a really fine act like that; because you can't—you simply *can't!*

Lady Rhoda (after a low whistle). No idea it had gone so far as that—already! *Now* I begin to see why Gerry Thicknesse has been lookin' as if he'd sat on his best hat, and why he told your aunt he might have to be off to-morrow; which is all stuff, because I happen to know his leave ain't up for two or three days yet. But he sees this Troubadour has put his poor old nose out of joint for him.

Lady Maisie (flushing). Now, Rhoda, I won't have you talking as if—as if—— *You* ought to know, if Gerald Thicknesse doesn't, that it's nothing at all of that sort! It's just—— Oh, I can't *tell* you how some of his poems moved me, what new ideas, wider views they seemed to teach; and then how *dreadfully* it hurt to think it was only Mr. Spurrell after all! . . . But *now*—oh, the *relief* of finding they're not spoilt; that I can still admire, still look up to

the man who wrote them! Not to have to feel that
he is quite commonplace—not even a gentleman—in
the ordinary sense!

Lady Rhoda (*rising*). Ah well, I prefer a hero who
looks as if he had his hair cut, occasionally—but
then, I'm not romantic. He may be the paragon
you say; but if I was you, my dear, I wouldn't expect
too much of that young man—allow a margin for
shrinkage, don't you know. And now I think I'll turn
into my little crib, for I'm dead tired. Good night;
don't sit up late readin' poetry; it's my opinion
you've read quite enough as it is!   [*She goes.*

Lady Maisie (*alone, as she gazes dreamily into the
fire*). She doesn't in the *least* understand! She
actually suspects me of—— As if I could possibly
—or as if mamma would ever—even if *he*—— Oh,
how *silly* I am! . . . I don't care! I *am* glad I
haven't had to give up my ideal. I *should* like to
know him better. What harm is there in that?
And if Gerald chooses to go to-morrow, he must—
that's all. He isn't nearly so nice as he used to be;
and he has even *less* imagination than ever! I don't
think I *could* care for anybody so absolutely matter-
of-fact. And yet, only an hour ago I almost——
But that was *before!*

PART XXI

THE FEELINGS OF A MOTHER.

In the Morning Room. Time—*Sunday morning; just after breakfast.*

Captain Thicknesse (outside, to Tredwell). Dog-cart round, eh? everything in? All right—shan't be a minute. (*Entering.*) Hallo, Pilliner, you all alone here? (*He looks round disconcertedly.*) Don't happen to have seen Lady Maisie about?

Pilliner. Let me see—she *was* here a little while ago, I fancy. . . . Why? Do you want her?

Captain Thicknesse. No—only to say good-bye and that. I'm just off.

Pilliner. Off? To-day! You don't mean to tell me your chief is such an inconsiderate old ruffian as to expect you to travel back to your Tommies on the Sabbath! You could wait till to-morrow if you *wanted* to. Come now!

Captain Thicknesse. Perhaps — only, you see, I *don't* want to.

Pilliner. Well, tastes differ. I shouldn't call a cross-country journey in a slow train, with unlimited opportunities of studying the company's bye-laws and traffic arrangements at several admirably venti-lated junctions, the ideal method of spending a cheery Sunday, myself, that's all.   •

Captain Thicknesse (gloomily). Dare say it will be about as cheery as stoppin' on here, if it comes to that.

Pilliner. I admit we were most of us a wee bit chippy at breakfast. The bard conversed—I will say *that* for him—but he seemed to diffuse a gloom somehow. Shut you up once or twice in a manner that might almost be described as damned offensive.

Captain Thicknesse. Don't know what you all saw in what he said that was so amusin'. Confounded rude *I* thought it!

Pilliner. Don't think any one *was* amused—unless it was Lady Maisie. By the way, he might perhaps have selected a happier topic to hold forth to Sir Rupert on than the scandalous indifference of large landowners to the condition of the rural labourer. Poor dear old boy, he stood it wonderfully, con-sidering. Pity Lady Cantire breakfasted upstairs; she'd have enjoyed herself. However, he had a very good audience in little Lady Maisie.

Captain Thicknesse. I do hate a chap that jaws at breakfast. . . . *Where* did you say she was?

Lady Maisie's voice (outside, in conservatory). Yes, you really ought to see the orangery and the Elizabethan garden, Mr. Blair. If you will be on the terrace in about five minutes, I could take you round myself. I must go and see if I can get the keys first.

Pilliner. If you want to say good-bye, old fellow, now's your chance!

Captain Thicknesse. It — it don't matter. She's engaged. And, look here, you needn't mention that I was askin' for her.

Pilliner. Of course, old fellow, if you'd rather not. (*He glances at him.*) But I say, my dear old chap, if *that's* how it is with you, I don't quite see the sense of chucking it up *already*, don't you know. No earthly affair of mine, I know; still, if I *could* manage to stay on, I would, if I were *you.*

Captain Thicknesse. Hang it all, Pilliner, do you suppose *I* don't know when the game's up! If it was any *good* stayin' on—— And besides, I've said good-bye to Lady C., and all that. No, it's too late now.

Tredwell (at the door). Excuse me, sir, but if you're going by the 10.40, you haven't any too much time.

Pilliner (to himself, after Captain THICKNESSE *has hurried out).* Poor old chap, he does seem hard hit ! Pity he's not Lady Maisie's sort. Though what she can see in that long-haired beggar——! Wonder when Vivien Spelwane intends to come down ; never knew her miss breakfast before. . . . What's that rustling ? . . . Women ! I'll be off, or they'll nail me for church before I know it.

> [*He disappears hastily in the direction of the Smoking - room as* Lady CANTIRE *and* Mrs. CHATTERIS *enter.*

Lady Cantire. Nonsense, my dear, no walk at all ; the church is only just across the park. My brother Rupert always goes, and it pleases him to see the Wyvern pew as full as possible. I seldom feel equal to going myself, because I find the necessity of allowing pulpit inaccuracies to pass without a protest gets too much on my nerves ; but my daughter will accompany you. You'll have just time to run up and get your things on.

Mrs. Chatteris (with arch significance). I don't *fancy* I shall have the pleasure of your daughter's society this morning. I just met her going to get the garden keys ; I think she has promised to show the grounds to—— Well, I needn't mention *whom.* Oh dear me, I hope I'm not being indiscreet *again !*

"I'LL BE OFF, OR THEY'LL NAIL ME FOR CHURCH BEFORE I KNOW IT."

Lady Cantire. I make a point of never interfering with my daughter's proceedings, and you can easily understand how natural it is that such old friends as they have always been——

Mrs. Chatteris. Really? I *thought* they seemed to take a great pleasure in one another's society. It's quite romantic. But I must rush up and get my bonnet on if I'm to go to church. (*To herself, as she goes out.*) So she *was* "Lady Grisoline," after all! If I was her mother—— But dear Lady Cantire is so advanced about things.

Lady Cantire (*to herself*). Darling Maisie! He'll be Lord Dunderhead before very long. How sensible and sweet of her! And I was quite uneasy about them last night at dinner; they scarcely seemed to be talking to each other at all. But there's a great deal more in dear Maisie than one would imagine.

Sir Rupert (*outside*). We're rather proud of our church, Mr. Undershell—fine old monuments and brasses, if you care about that sort of thing. Some of us will be walking over to service presently, if you would like to——

Undershell (*outside — to himself*). And lose my *tête-à-tête* with Lady Maisie! Not exactly! (*Aloud.*) I am afraid, Sir Rupert, that I cannot conscientiously——

Sir Rupert (*hastily*). Oh, very well, very well; do exactly as you like about it, of course. I only thought—— (*To himself.*) Now, that *other* young chap would have gone!

Lady Cantire. Rupert, who is that you are talking to out there? I don't recognise his voice, somehow.

Sir Rupert (*entering with* UNDERSHELL). Ha, Rohesia, you've come down, then? slept well, I hope. I was talking to a gentleman whose acquaintance I know you will be very happy to make—at last. This is the genuine celebrity *this* time. (*To* UNDERSHELL.) Let me make you known to my sister, Lady Cantire, Mr. Undershell. (*As* Lady CANTIRE *glares interrogatively.*) Mr. Clarion Blair, Rohesia, author of hum—ha—*Andromache*.

Lady Cantire. I thought we were given to understand last night that Mr. Spurrell—Mr. Blair—you must pardon me, but it's really so very confusing—that the writer of the—ah—volume in question had already left Wyvern.

Sir Rupert. Well, my dear, you see he is still here—er—fortunately for us. If you'll excuse me, I'll leave Mr. Blair to entertain you; got to speak to Adams about something.   [*He hurries out.*

Undershell (*to himself*). This must be Lady Maisie's mamma. Better be civil to her, I suppose;

but I can't stay here and entertain her long!
(*Aloud.*) Lady Cantire, I—er—have an appointment for which I am already a little late ; but
before I go, I should like to tell you how much
pleasure it has given me to know that my poor
verse has won your approval ; appreciation from——

Lady Cantire. I'm afraid you must have been
misinformed, Mr.—a—Blair.   There are so many
serious publications claiming attention in these days
of literary over-production that I have long made it
a rule to read no literature of a lighter order that has
not been before the world for at least ten years.   I
may be mistaken, but I infer from your appearance
that your own work must be of a considerably more
recent date.

Undershell (*to himself*). If she imagines she's
going to snub Me—— ! (*Aloud.*) Then I was
evidently mistaken in gathering from some expres-
sions in your daughter's letter that——

Lady Cantire. Entirely. You are probably thinking of some totally different person, as my daughter
has never mentioned having written to you, and is
not in the habit of conducting *any* correspondence
without my full knowledge and approval.   I think
you said you had some appointment ; if so, pray don't
consider yourself under any necessity to remain here.

Undershell. You are very good; I will not. (*To himself, as he retires.*) Awful old lady, that! I quite thought she would know all about that letter, or I should never have—— However, I said nothing to compromise any one, luckily!

Lady Culverin (*entering*). Good morning, Rohesia. So glad you felt equal to coming down. I was almost afraid—after *last night*, you know.

Lady Cantire (*offering a cold cheekbone for salutation*). I am in my usual health, thank you, Albinia. As to last night, if you *must* ask a literary Socialist down here, you might at least see that he is received with common courtesy. You may, for anything *you* can tell, have advanced the Social Revolution ten years in a single evening!

Lady Culverin. My *dear* Rohesia! If you remember, it was you yourself who——!

Lady Cantire (*closing her eyes*). I am in no condition to *argue* about it, Albinia. The slightest exercise of your own common sense would have shown you—— But there, no great harm has been done, fortunately, so let us say no more about it. I have something more agreeable to talk about. I've every reason to hope that Maisie and dear Gerald Thicknesse——

Lady Culverin (*astonished*). Maisie? But I thought Gerald Thicknesse spoke as if——!

Lady Cantire. Very possibly, my dear. I have always refrained from giving him the slightest encouragement, and I wouldn't put any pressure upon dear Maisie for the world—still, I have my feelings as a mother, and I can't deny that, with such prospects as he has´ now, it *is* gratifying for me to think that they may be coming to an understanding together at this very moment. She is showing him the grounds; which I always think are the great charm of Wyvern, so *secluded!*

Lady Culverin (puzzled). Together! At this very moment! But—but surely Gerald has *gone?*

Lady Cantire. Gone! What nonsense, Albinia! Where in the world should he have gone to?

Lady Culverin. He *was* leaving by the 10.40, I know. For Aldershot. I ordered the cart for him, and he said good-bye after breakfast. He seemed so dreadfully down, poor fellow, and I quite concluded from what he said that Maisie must have——

Lady Cantire. Impossible, my dear, quite impossible! I tell you he is *here.* Why, only a few minutes ago, Mrs. Chatteris was telling me—— Ah, here she is to speak for herself. (*To* Mrs. Chatteris, *who appears, arrayed for divine service.*) Mrs. Chatteris, did I, or did I *not,* understand you to say just now that my daughter Maisie—— ?

Mrs. Chatteris (*alarmed*). But, *dear* Lady Cantire, I had no idea you would disapprove. Indeed you seemed—— And really, though she certainly seems to find him rather well—*sympathetic*—I'm sure—*almost* sure — there can be nothing serious — at present.

Lady Cantire. Thank you, my dear, I merely wished for an answer to my question. And you see, Albinia, that Gerald Thicknesse can hardly have gone yet, since he is walking about the grounds with Maisie.

Mrs. Chatteris. Captain Thicknesse? But he *has* gone, Lady Cantire! I saw him start. I didn't mean *him*.

Lady Cantire. Indeed? then I shall be obliged if you will say who it is you *did* mean.

Mrs. Chatteris. Why, only her old friend and admirer—that little poet man, Mr. Blair.

Lady Cantire (*to herself*). And I actually *sent* him to her! (*Rising in majestic wrath.*) Albinia, whatever comes of this, remember I shall hold *you* entirely responsible!

     [*She sweeps out of the room; the other two ladies look after her, and then at one another, in silent consternation.*

PART XXII

A DESCENT FROM THE CLOUDS

In the Elizabethan Garden. Lady MAISIE *and* UNDERSHELL *are on a seat in the Yew Walk.* TIME—*About* 11 A.M.

Lady Maisie (softly). And you really meant to go away, and never let one of us know what had happened to you!

Undershell (to himself). How easy it is after all to be a hero! (*Aloud.*) That certainly *was* my intention, only I was—er—not permitted to carry it out. I trust you don't consider I should have been to blame?

Lady Maisie (with shining eyes). To *blame?* Mr. Blair! As if I could possibly do that! (*To herself.*) He doesn't even see *how* splendid it was of him!

Undershell (to himself). I begin to believe that I can do *no* wrong in her eyes! (*Aloud.*) It was not altogether easy, believe me, to leave without even having seen your face; but I felt so strongly that it was better so.

Lady Maisie (*looking down*). And—do you still feel that?

Undershell. I must confess that I am well content to have failed. It was such unspeakable torture to think that you, Lady Maisie, *you* of all people, would derive your sole idea of my personality from such an irredeemable vulgarian as that veterinary surgeon —the man Spurrell!

Lady Maisie (*to herself, with an almost imperceptible start*). I suppose it's only natural he should feel like that—but I wish—I *do* wish he had put it just a little differently! (*Aloud.*) Poor Mr. Spurrell! perhaps he was not exactly——

Undershell. **Not** *exactly!* I assure you it is simply inconceivable to me that, in a circle of any pretensions to culture and refinement, an ill-bred boor like that could have been accepted for a single moment as—I won't say a Man of *Genius,* but——

Lady Maisie (*the light dying out of her eyes*). No, *don't*—don't go on, Mr. Blair. We were all excessively stupid, no doubt, but you must make allowances for us—for *me*, especially. I have had so few opportunities of meeting people who are really distinguished—in literature, at least. Most of the people I know best are—well, not exactly *clever,* you know. I so often wish I was in a set that cared rather more about intellectual things!

Undershell (*with infinite pity*). How you must have pined for freer air! How you must have starved on such mental provender as, for example, the vapid and inane commonplaces of that swaggering carpet-soldier, Captain—Thickset, isn't it?

Lady Maisie (*drawing back into her corner*). You evidently don't know that Captain Thicknesse distinguished himself greatly in the Soudan, where he was very severely wounded.

Undershell. Possibly; but that is scarcely to the point. I do not question his efficiency as a fighting animal. As to his intelligence, perhaps, the less said the better.

Lady Maisie (*contracting her brows*). Decidedly. I ought to have mentioned at once that Captain Thicknesse is a very old friend of mine.

Undershell. Really? *He*, at least, may be congratulated. But pray don't think that I spoke with any personal animus; I merely happen to entertain a peculiar aversion for a class whose profession is systematic slaughter. In these Democratic times, when Humanity is advancing by leaps and bounds towards International Solidarity, soldiers are such grotesque and unnecessary anachronisms.

Lady Maisie (*to herself, with a little shiver*). Oh, why does he—why *does* he? (*Aloud.*) I should have thought that, until war itself is an anachronism, men who are willing to fight and die for their country could never be quite unnecessary. But we won't discuss Captain Thicknesse, particularly now that he has left Wyvern. Suppose we go back to Mr. Spurrell. I know, of course, that, in leaving him in ignorance as you did, you acted from the best and highest motives; but still——

Undershell. It is refreshing to be so thoroughly understood! I think I know what your "but still" implies—why did I not foresee that he would infallibly betray himself before long? I *did*. But I gave him credit for being able to sustain his part for another hour or two—until I had gone, in fact.

Lady Maisie. Then you didn't wish to spare *his* feelings as well as ours?

Undershell. To be quite frank, I didn't trouble myself about him: my sole object was to retreat with dignity; he had got himself somehow or other into a false position he must get out of as best he could. After all, he would be none the worse for having filled *my* place for a few hours.

Lady Maisie (*slowly*). I see. It didn't matter to you whether he was suspected of being an impostor,

or made to feel uncomfortable, or—or anything.
Wasn't that a little unfeeling of you?

Undershell. Unfeeling! I allowed him to keep
my evening clothes, which is more than a good
many——

Lady Maisie. At all events, he may have had to
pay more heavily than you imagine. I wonder
whether—— But I suppose anything so unroman-
tic as the love affairs of a veterinary surgeon would
have no interest for you?

Undershell. Why not, Lady Maisie? To the
Student of Humanity, and still more to the Poet,
the humblest love-story may have its interesting—
even its suggestive—aspect.

Lady Maisie. Well, I may tell you that it seems
Mr. Spurrell has long been attached, if not actually
engaged, to a maid of mine.

Undershell (startled out of his self-possession). You
—you don't mean to Miss Phillipson?

Lady Maisie. That *is* her name. How very odd
that you—— But perhaps Mr. Spurrell mentioned
it to you last night?

Undershell (recovering his sangfroid). I am hardly
likely to have heard of it from any other quarter.

Lady Maisie. Of course not. And did he tell you
that she was here, in this very house?

Undershell. No, he never mentioned *that.* What a remarkable coincidence!

Lady Maisie. Yes, rather.   The worst of it is that the foolish girl seems to have heard that he was a guest here, and have jumped to the conclusion that he had ceased to care for her; so she revenged herself by a desperate flirtation with some worthless wretch she met in the housekeeper's room, whose flattery and admiration, I'm very much afraid, have completely turned her head!

Undershell (*uncomfortably*). Ah, well, she must learn to forget him, and no doubt, in time—— How wonderful the pale sunlight is on that yew hedge!

Lady Maisie. You are not very sympathetic!   I should not have told you at all, only I wanted to show you that if poor Mr. Spurrell *did* innocently usurp your place, he may have lost—— But I see all this only bores you.

Undershell. Candidly, Lady Maisie, I can't affect a very keen interest in the—er—gossip of the house-keeper's room.   Indeed, I am rather surprised that *you* should condescend to listen to——

Lady Maisie (*to herself*). This is really *too* much! (*Aloud.*) It never occurred to me that I was "con-descending" in taking an interest in a pretty and wayward girl who happens to be my maid. But then, I'm not a Democrat, Mr. Blair.

Undershell. I—I'm afraid you construed my remark as a rebuke; which it was not at all intended to be.

Lady Maisie. It would have been rather super-fluous if it had been, wouldn't it? (*Observing his growing uneasiness.*) I'm afraid you don't find this bench quite comfortable?

Undershell. I—er—moderately so. (*To himself.*) There's a female figure coming down the terrace steps. It's horribly like—— But that must be my morbid fancy; still, if I can get Lady Maisie away, just in case—— (*Aloud.*) D—don't you think sitting still becomes a little—er—monotonous after a time? Couldn't we—— [*He rises, spasmodically.*

Lady Maisie (*rising too*). Certainly; we have sat here quite long enough. It is time we went back.

Undershell (*to himself*). We shall meet her! and I'm almost sure it's—— I *must* prevent any—— (*Aloud.*) Not *back*, Lady Maisie! You—you pro-mised to show me the orchid-house—you did, indeed!

Lady Maisie. Very well; we can go in, if you care about orchids. It's on our way back.

Undershell (*to himself*). This is too awful! It *is* that girl Phillipson. She is looking for somebody!

Me! (*Aloud.*) On second thoughts, I don't think I *do* care to see the orchids. I detest them; they are such weird, unnatural, extravagant things. Let us turn back and see if there are any snowdrops on the lawn behind that hedge. I love the snowdrop, it is so trustful and innocent, with its pure green-veined—— *Do* come and search for snowdrops!

Lady Maisie. Not just now. I think—(*as she shields her eyes with one hand*)—I'm not quite sure yet—but I rather fancy that must be my maid at the other end of the walk.

Undershell (*eagerly*). *I* assure you, Lady Maisie, you are quite mistaken. Not the *least* like her!

Lady Maisie (*astonished*). Why, how can you possibly tell that, without having seen her, Mr. Blair?

Undershell. I—I meant—— You described her as "pretty," you know. This girl is plain—distinctly plain!

Lady Maisie. I don't agree at all. However, it certainly is Phillipson, and she seems to have come out in search of me; so I had better see if she has any message.

Undershell. She hasn't. I'm *positive* she hasn't. She—she wouldn't walk like *that* if she had. (*In feverish anxiety.*) Lady Maisie, shall we turn back? She—she hasn't seen us *yet!*

"DO COME AND SEARCH FOR SNOWDROPS!"

Lady Maisie. Really, Mr. Blair! I don't quite see why I should run away from my own maid! . . . What is it, Phillipson?

[*She advances to meet* PHILLIPSON, *leaving* UNDERSHELL *behind, motionless.*

Undershell (*to himself*). It's all over! That confounded girl recognises me. I saw her face change! She'll be jealous, I *know* she'll be jealous—and then she'll tell Lady Maisie everything! . . . I wish to Heaven I could hear what she is saying. Lady Maisie seems agitated. . . . I—I might stroll gently on and leave them; but it would look too like running away, perhaps. No, I'll stay here and face it out like a man! I won't give up just yet. (*He sinks limply upon the bench.*) After all, I've been in worse holes than this since I came into this infernal place, and I've always managed to scramble out— triumphantly too! If she will only give me five minutes alone, I *know* I can clear myself; it isn't as if I had done anything to be *ashamed* of. . . . She's sent away that girl. She seems to be expecting me to come to her. . . . I—I suppose I'd better.

[*He rises with effort, and goes towards* Lady MAISIE **with a jaunty unconsciousness that** *somehow has the air of stopping short just* **above the knees.**

PART XXIII

SHRINKAGE

In the Yew Walk.

Lady Maisie (to herself, as she watches UNDERSHELL *approaching).* How badly he walks, and what *does* he mean by smiling at me like that? (*Aloud, coldly.*) I am sorry, Mr. Blair, but I must leave you to finish your stroll alone; my maid has just told me——

Undershell (vehemently). Lady Maisie, I ask you, in common fairness, not to judge me until you have heard *my* version. You will not allow the fact that I travelled down here in the same compartment with your maid, Phillipson——

Lady Maisie (wide-eyed). The *same!* But *we* came by that train. I thought you missed it?

Undershell. I—I was not so fortunate. It is rather a long and complicated story, but——

Lady Maisie. I'm afraid I really can't listen to you *now*, Mr. Blair, after what I have heard from Phillipson——

Undershell. I implore you not to go without hearing both sides. Sit down again—if only for a minute. I feel confident that I can explain everything satisfactorily.

Lady Maisie (sitting down). I can't imagine what there is to explain—and really I ought, if Phillipson——

Undershell. You know what maids *are*, Lady Maisie. They embroider. Unintentionally, I dare say, but still, they *do* embroider.

Lady Maisie (puzzled). She is very clever at mending lace, I know, though what *that* has to do with it——

Undershell. Listen to me, Lady Maisie. I came to this house at your bidding. Yes, but for your written appeal, I should have treated the invitation I received from your aunt with silent contempt. Had I obeyed my first impulse and ignored it, I should have been spared humiliations and indignities which ought rather to excite your pity than—than any other sensation. Think—try to realise what my feelings must have been when I found myself expected by the butler here to sit down to supper with him and the upper servants in the housekeeper's room!

Lady Maisie (shocked). Oh, Mr. Blair! Indeed, I had no—— You weren't *really!* How *could* they? What *did* you say?

Undershell (*haughtily*). I believe I let him know my opinion of the snobbery of his employers in treating a guest of theirs so cavalierly.

Lady Maisie (*distressed*). But surely—*surely* you couldn't suppose that my uncle and aunt were capable of——

Undershell. What else *could* I suppose, under the circumstances? It is true I have since learnt that I was mistaken in this particular instance; but I am not ignorant of the ingrained contempt you aristocrats have for all who live by exercising their intellect—the bitter scorn of birth for brains!

Lady Maisie. I am afraid the—the contempt is all on the other side; but if *that* is how you feel about it, I don't wonder that you were indignant.

Undershell. Indignant! I was *furious*. In fact, nothing would have induced me to sit down to supper at all, if it hadn't been for——

Lady Maisie (*in a small voice*). Then—you *did* sit down? With the servants! Oh, Mr. Blair!

Undershell. I thought you were already aware of it. Yes, Lady Maisie, I endured even that. But (*with magnanimity*) you must not distress yourself about it now. If *I* can forget it, surely you can do so!

Lady Maisie. Can I? That *you* should have

consented, for any consideration whatever; how could you—how *could* you?

Undershell (to himself). She admires me all the more for it. But I *knew* she would take the right view! (*Aloud, with pathos.*) I was only compelled by absolute starvation. I had had an unusually light lunch, and I was so hungry!

Lady Maisie (after a pause). That explains it, of course. . . . I hope they gave you a good supper!

Undershell. Excellent, thank you. Indeed, I was astonished at the variety and even luxury of the table. There was a pyramid of quails——

Lady Maisie. I am pleased to hear it. But I thought there was something you were going to explain.

Undershell. I have been *endeavouring* to explain to the best of my ability that if I have undesignedly been the cause of—er—a temporary diversion in the state of Miss Phillipson's affections, no one could regret more deeply than I that the—er—ordinary amenities of the supper-table should have been mistaken for——

Lady Maisie (horrified). Oh, stop, Mr. Blair, please stop! I don't want to hear any more. I see now. It was *you* who——

Undershell. Of course it was I. Surely the girl herself has been telling you so just now!

Lady Maisie. You really thought *that* possible, too? She simply came with a message from my mother.

Undershell (*slightly disconcerted*). Oh! If I had known it was merely *that.* However, I am sure I need not ask you to treat my—my communication in the strictest confidence, Lady Maisie.

Lady Maisie. Indeed, that is *perfectly* unnecessary, Mr. Blair.

Undershell. Yes, I felt from the first that I could trust you—even with my life. And I cannot regret having told you, if it has enabled you to understand me more thoroughly. It is such a relief that you know all, and that there are no more secrets between us. You *do* feel that I only acted as was natural and inevitable under the circumstances?

Lady Maisie. Oh yes, yes. I—I dare say you could not help it. I mean you did quite, *quite* right!

Undershell. Ah, how you comfort me with your fresh girlish—— You are not *going*, Lady Maisie?

Lady Maisie (*rising*). I must. I ought to have gone before. My mother wants me. No, you are not to come too; you can go on and gather those snowdrops, you know.

[*She walks slowly back to the house.*

Undershell (*looking after her*). She took it wonder-fully well. I've made it all right, or she wouldn't have said that about the snowdrops. Yes, she shall not be disappointed; she shall have her posy!

In the Morning-room. Half an hour later.

Lady Maisie (*alone—to herself*). Thank goodness, *that's* over! It was *awful*. I don't think I *ever* saw mamma a deeper shade of plum colour! *How* I have been mistaken in Mr. Blair! That he could write those lines—

> "Aspiring unto that far-off Ideal,
> I may not stoop to any meaner love,"

and yet philander with my poor foolish Phillipson the moment he met her! And then to tell mamma about my letter like that! Why, even Mr. Spurrell had more discretion—to be sure, *he* knew nothing about it—but *that* makes no difference! Rhoda was right; I ought to have allowed a margin—only I should never have allowed margin *enough!* The worst of it is that, if mamma was unjust in some things she said, she was right about *one*. I *have* disgusted Gerald. He mayn't be brilliant, but at least he's straightforward and loyal and a gentleman, and—and he *did* like me once. He doesn't any more—or he wouldn't have gone away. And it may be ages before I ever get a chance to let him see how *dreadfully* sorry—— (*She turns, and sees* Captain THICKNESSE.) Oh, haven't you gone *yet?*

Captain Thicknesse. Yes, I went, but I've come back again. I—I couldn't help it; 'pon my word I couldn't.

Lady Maisie (*with a sudden flush*). You—you weren't *sent* for—by—by any one?

Captain Thicknesse. So *likely* any one would send for me, isn't it?

Lady Maisie. I don't know why I said that; it was silly, of course. But how——

Captain Thicknesse. Ran it a bit too fine; got to Shuntin'bridge just in time to see the tail end of the train disappearin'; wasn't another for hours—not much to do *there*, don't you know.

Lady Maisie. You might have taken a walk—or gone to church.

Captain Thicknesse. So I might, didn't occur to me; and besides, I—I remembered I never said good-bye to *you.*

Lady. Maisie. Didn't you? And whose fault was that?

Captain Thicknesse. Not mine, anyhow. You were somewhere about the grounds with Mr. Blair.

Lady Maisie. Now you mention it, I believe I

was. We had—rather an interesting conversation. Still, you might have come to look for me!

Captain Thicknesse. Perhaps you wouldn't have been over and above glad to see me.

Lady Maisie. Oh yes, I should!—When it was to say *good-bye*, you know!

·Captain Thicknesse. Ah! Well, I suppose I shall only be in the way if I stop here any longer now.

Lady Maisie. Do you? What makes you suppose that?

Captain Thicknesse. Nothin'! Saw your friend the bard hurryin' along the terrace with a bunch of snowdrops; he'll be here in another——

Lady Maisie (in unmistakable horror). Gerald, *why* didn't you tell me before? There's only just time! *[She flies to a door and opens it.*

Captain Thicknesse. But I *say*, you know! Maisie, may I come too?

Lady Maisie. Don't be a *goose*, Gerald. Of course you can, if you like.

[She disappears in the conservatory.

Captain Thicknesse (to himself). Can't quite make this out, but I'm no end glad I came back!

[He follows quickly.

Undershell (entering). I hoped I should find her here. *(He looks round.)* Her mother's gone—that's

R

something! I dare say Lady Maisie will come in presently. (*He sits down and re-arranges his snow-drops.*) It will be sweet to see her face light up when I offer her these as a symbol of the new and closer link between us! (*He hears the sound of drapery behind him.*) Ah, already! (*Rising, and presenting his flowers with downcast eyes.*) I—I have ventured to gather these—for you. (*He raises his eyes.* Miss Spelwane!

Miss Spelwane (*taking them graciously*). How very sweet of you, Mr. Blair. Are they really for me?

Undershell (*concealing his disappointment*). Oh—er —yes. If you will give me the pleasure of accepting them.

Miss Spelwane. I feel immensely proud. I was so afraid you must have thought I was rather cross to you last night. I didn't mean to be. I was feeling a little overdone, that was all. But you have chosen a charming way of letting me see that I am forgiven. (*To herself.*) It's really *too* touching. He certainly is a great improvement on the other wretch!

Undershell (*dolefully*). I—I had no such intention, I assure you. (*To himself.*) I hope to goodness Lady Maisie won't come in before I can get rid of this girl. I seem fated to be misunderstood here!

"HOW VERY SWEET OF YOU, MR. BLAIR. ARE THEY REALLY FOR ME?"

PART XXIV

THE HAPPY DISPATCH

"Perhaps it was right to dissemble your love, but——"

In the Morning-room. TIME—*About* 1 P.M.

Undershell (*to himself alone*). I'm rather sorry that
that Miss Spelwane couldn't stay. She's a trifle
angular—but clever. It was distinctly sharp of her
to see through that fellow Spurrell from the first,
and lay such an ingenious little trap for him. And
she has a great feeling for Literature—knows my
verses by heart, I discovered, quite accidentally. All
the same, I wish she hadn't intercepted those snowdrops. Now I shall have to go out and pick some
more. (*Sounds outside in the entrance hall.*) Too
late—they've got back from church!

Mrs. Brooke-Chatteris (*entering with* Lady RHODA,
Sir RUPERT *and* BEARPARK). Such a nice, plain,
simple service—I'm positively *ravenous!*

Lady Rhoda. Struck me some of those chubby
choir-boys wanted smackin'. What a business it
seems to get the servants properly into their pew—

as bad as boxin' a string of hunters! As for *you*,
Archie, the way you fidgeted durin' the sermon was
downright disgraceful! . . . So *there* you are, Mr.
Blair; not been to church; but I forgot—p'raps you're
a Dissenter, or somethin'?

Undershell (*annoyed*). Only, Lady Rhoda, in the
sense that I have hitherto failed to discover any form
of creed that commands my intellectual assent.

Lady Rhoda (*unimpressed*). I expect you haven't
tried. Are you a—what d'ye call it?—a Lacedemoniac?

Undershell (*with lofty tolerance*). I *presume* you
mean a "Laodicean." No, I should rather describe
myself as a Deist.

Archie (*in a surly undertone*). What's a *Deast*
when he's at home? If he'd said a *Beast*, now!
(*Aloud, as* PILLINER *enters with* Captain THICKNESSE.)
Hullo, why, here's Thicknesse! So you *haven't* gone,
after all, then?

Captain Thicknesse. What an observant young
beggar you are, Bearpark! Nothin' escapes you.
No, I haven't. (*To* Sir RUPERT, *rather sheepishly.*)
Fact, is, sir, I—I somehow just missed the train,
and—and—thought I might as well come back,
instead of waitin' about, don't you know.

Sir Rupert (*heartily*). Why, of course, my dear
boy, of course! Never have forgiven you if you

hadn't. Great nuisance for *you*, though. Hope you blew the fool of a man up; he *ought* to have been round in plenty of time.

Captain Thicknesse. Not the groom's fault, sir. I kept him waitin' a bit, and—and we had to stop to shift the seat and that, and so——

Undershell (*to himself*). Great blundering booby! Can't he see nobody wants him *here*? As if he hadn't bored poor Lady Maisie enough at breakfast! Ah, well, I must come to her rescue once more, I suppose!

Sir Rupert. Half an hour to lunch! Anybody like to come round to the stables? I'm going to see how my wife's horse Deerfoot is getting on. Fond of horses, eh, Mr.—a—Undershell? Care to come with us?

Undershell (*to himself*). I've seen quite enough of *that* beast already! (*Aloud, with some asperity.*) You must really excuse me, Sir Rupert. I am at one with Mr. Ruskin—I *detest* horses.

Sir Rupert. Ah? Pity. We're rather fond of 'em here. But we can't expect a poet to be a sportsman, eh?

Undershell. For my own poor part, I confess I look forward to a day, not far distant, when the spread of civilisation will have abolished every form of so-called Sport.

Sir Rupert. Do you, though? (*After conquering a choke with difficulty.*) Allow me to hope that you will continue to enjoy the pleasures of anticipation as long as possible. (*To the rest.*) Well, are you coming? [*All except* UNDERSHELL *follow their host out.*

Undershell (*alone, to himself*). If they think I'm going to be *patronised*, or suppress my honest convictions——! Now I'll go and pick those—— (Lady MAISIE *enters from the conservatory.*) Ah, Lady Maisie, I have been trying to find you. I had plucked a few snowdrops, which I promised myself the pleasure of presenting to you. Unfortunately they—er—failed to reach their destination.

Lady Maisie (*distantly*). Thanks, Mr. Blair; I am only sorry you should have given yourself such unnecessary trouble.

Undershell (*detaining her, as she seemed about to pass on*). I have another piece of intelligence which you may hear less—er—philosophically, Lady Maisie. Your *bête noire* has returned.

Lady Maisie (*with lifted eyebrows*). My *bête noire*, Mr. Blair?

Undershell. Why affect not to understand? I have an infallible instinct in all matters concerning *you*, and, sweetly tolerant as you are, I instantly divined what an insufferable nuisance you found our military friend, Captain Thicknesse.

Lady Maisie. There are limits even to *my* tolerance,

Mr. Blair.   I admit I find some people insufferable
—but Captain Thicknesse is not one of them.

Undershell. Then appearances are deceptive indeed.
Come, Lady Maisie, surely you can trust *me!*

[Lady CANTIRE *enters.*

Lady Cantire (*in her most awful tones*). Maisie, my
dear, I appear to have interrupted an interview of a
somewhat confidential character.   If so, pray let me
know it, and I will go elsewhere.

Lady Maisie (*calmly*). Not in the very least,
mamma.   Mr. Blair was merely trying to prepare
me for the fact that Captain Thicknesse has come
back; which was quite needless, as I happen to have
heard it already from his own lips.

Lady Cantire. Captain Thicknesse come back!
(*To* UNDERSHELL.)   I wish to speak to my daughter.
May I ask you to leave us ?

Undershell. With pleasure, Lady Cantire.   (*To
himself, as he retires.*)   What a consummate actress
that girl is!   And what a coquette!

Lady Cantire (*after a silence*). Maisie, what does
all this mean ?   No *nonsense,* now!   What brought
Gerald Thicknesse back ?

Lady Maisie. I *suppose* the dog-cart, mamma.   He
missed his train, you know.   I don't think he minds
—much.

Lady Cantire. Let me tell you *this*, my dear. It is a great deal more than you *deserve* after—— How long has he come back for?

Lady Maisie. Only a few hours; but—but from things he said, I fancy he would stay on longer—if Aunt Albinia asked him.

Lady Cantire. Then we may consider that settled; he stays. (Lady CULVERIN *appears.*) Here *is* your aunt. You had better leave us, my dear.

Somewhat later; the Party have assembled for Lunch.

Sir Rupert (to his wife). Well, my dear, I've seen that young Spurrell (smart fellow he is, too, thoroughly up in his business), and you'll be glad to hear he can't find anything seriously wrong with Deerfoot.

Undershell (in the background, to himself). No more could I, for that matter!

Sir Rupert. He's clear it isn't navicular, which Adams was afraid of, and he thinks, with care and rest, you know, the horse will be as fit as a fiddle in a very few days.

Undershell (to himself). Just exactly what I *told* them; but the fools wouldn't believe *me!*

Lady Culverin. Oh, Rupert, I *am* so glad. How clever of that nice Mr. Spurrell! I was afraid my poor Deerfoot would have to be shot.

Undershell (*to himself*). She may thank me that he *wasn't*. And this other fellow gets all the credit for it. How like Life!

Lady Maisie. And, Uncle Rupert, how about—about Phillipson, you know? Is it all right?

Sir Rupert. Phillipson? Oh, why, 'pon my word, my dear, didn't think of asking.

Lady Rhoda. But *I* did, Maisie. And they met this mornin', and it's all settled, and they're as happy as they can be. Except that he's on the look out for a mysterious stranger, who disappeared last night, after tryin' to make desperate love to her. He is determined, if he can find him, to give him a piece of his mind.

> [UNDERSHELL *endeavours to conceal his extreme uneasiness.*

Pilliner. And the whole of a horsewhip. He invited my opinion of it as an implement of castigation. Kind of thing, you know, that would impart "proficiency in the *trois temps*, as danced in the most select circles," in a single lesson to a lame bear. (*To himself.*) I drew my little bow at a venture, and I'm hanged if it hasn't touched him up! There's *something* fishy about this chap—I felt it all along. Still, I don't see what more I can do—or I'd do it, for poor old Gerry Thicknesse's sake.

Undershell (*to himself*). I don't stir a step out of this house while I'm here, that's all!

Sir Rupert. Ha-ha! Athletic young chap that. Glad to see him in the field next Tuesday. By the way, Albinia, you've heard how Thicknesse here contrived to miss his train this morning? Our gain, of course; but still we must manage to get you back to Aldershot to-night, my boy, or you'll get called over the coals by your colonel when you *do* put in an appearance, hey? Now, let's see; what train ought you to catch?

> [*He takes up* "Bradshaw" *from a writing-table.*

Lady Cantire (*possessing herself of the volume*). Allow me, Rupert, my eyes are better than yours. *I* will look out his trains for him. (*After consulting various pages.*) Just as I *thought!* Quite impossible for him to reach North Camp to-night now. There isn't a train till six, and *that* gets to town just too late for him to drive across to Waterloo and catch the last Aldershot train. So there's no more to be said. [*She puts* "Bradshaw" *away.*

Captain Thicknesse (*with undisguised relief*). Oh, well, dessay they won't kick up much of a row if I don't get back till to-morrow,—or the day *after*, if it comes to that.

Undershell (*to himself*). It *shan't* come to that—if *I* can prevent it! Lady Maisie is quite in despair, I can see. (*Aloud.*) Indeed? I was—a—not aware that discipline was quite so lax as that in the British Army. And surely officers should set an example of——

> [*He finds that his intervention has produced a distinct sensation, and, taking up the discarded "Bradshaw" becomes engrossed in its study.*

Captain Thicknesse (*ignoring him completely*). It's like this, Lady Culverin. Somehow I—I muddled up the dates, don't you know. Mean to say, got it into my head to-day was the 20th, instead of only the 18th. (*Lamely.*) That's how it *was*.

Lady Culverin. Delightful, my dear Gerald. Then we shall keep you here till Tuesday, of *course!*

Undershell (*looking up from "Bradshaw," impulsively*). Lady Culverin, I see there's a very good train which leaves Shuntingbridge at 3.15 this afternoon, and gets——

> [*The rest regard him with unaffected surprise and disapproval.*

Lady Cantire (*raising her glasses*). Upon my word, Mr. Blair! If you will kindly leave Captain Thicknesse to make his own arrangements——!

Lady Maisie (*interposing hastily*). But, mamma, you must have misunderstood Mr. Blair! As if he would *dream* of—— He was merely mentioning the train he wishes to go by himself. *Weren't* you, Mr. Blair?

Undershell (*blinking and gasping*). I—eh? Just so, that—that *was* my intention, certainly. (*To himself.*) Does she at all realise what this will cost her?

Lady Culverin. My dear Mr. Blair, I—I'd no notion we were to lose you so soon; but if you're really quite *sure* you must go——

Lady Cantire (*sharply*). Really, Albinia, we must give him credit for knowing his own mind. He tells you he is *obliged to go!*

Lady Culverin. Then of course we must let you do *exactly* as you please.

Pilliner (*to himself*). Lady Maisie's a little brick! No notion she had it *in* her. No occasion to bother myself about the beggar now. "Let him alone and he'll go home, and carry his tail beneath him!"

[*All except* Miss SPELWANE *breathe more freely;*
TREDWELL *appears.*

Lady Culverin. Oh, lunch, is it, Tredwell? Very well. By the bye, see that some one packs Mr. Undershell's things for him, and tell them to send

the dog-cart round after lunch in time to catch the
3.15 from Shuntingbridge.

Archie (sotto voce, to PILLINER). We don't want any
more missin' of trains, eh? I'll go round and see
the cart properly balanced myself *this* time.

Pilliner (in the same tone). No, dear boy, you're
not to be trusted! *I'll* see that done, then the bard
and his train will be alike in one respect—*neither* of
'em 'll be missed!

Miss Spelwane (to herself, piqued.) Going already!
I wish I had never touched his ridiculous snowdrops!

Lady Culverin. Well, shall we go in to lunch,
everybody?

> [*They move in irregular order towards the
> dining-hall.*

Undershell (in an undertone to Lady MAISIE, *as
they follow last).* Lady Maisie, I—er—this is just a
little unexpected. I confess I don't quite understand
your precise motive in suggesting so—so hasty a
departure.

Lady Maisie (without looking at him). Don't you,
Mr. Blair? Perhaps—when you come to think over
it all quietly—you *will*.

> [*She passes on, leaving him perplexed.*

Undershell (to himself). Shall I? I certainly can't
say I do just—— Why, yes, I *do!* That bully

"PERHAPS—WHEN YOU COME TO THINK OVER IT ALL QUIETLY—YOU WILL."

Spurrell with his horsewhip! She dreads an encounter between us—and I should much prefer to avoid it myself. Yes; that's it, of course. She is willing to sacrifice anything rather than endanger *my* personal safety! What unselfish angels some women are! Even that sneering fellow Drysdale will be impressed when I tell him this. . . . Yes, it's best that I should go—I see that now. I don't so much mind leaving. Without any false humility, I can hardly avoid seeing that, even in the short time I have been amongst these people, I have produced a decided impression. And there is at least one—perhaps *two*—who will miss me when I am gone.

[*He goes into the Dining-hall, with restored complacency.*

THE END.

PRINTED BY WILLIAM CLOWES AND SONS, LIMITED, LONDON AND BECCLES.

WORKS BY F. ANSTEY.

THE TALKING HORSE;
AND OTHER TALES.

From THE SATURDAY REVIEW.—"A capital set of stories, thoroughly clever and witty, often pathetic, and always humorous."

From THE ATHENÆUM.—"The grimmest of mortals, in his most surly mood, could hardly resist the fun of 'The Talking Horse.'"

THE GIANT'S ROBE.

From THE PALL MALL GAZETTE.—"The main interest of the book, which is very strong indeed, begins when Vincent returns, when Harold Caffyn discovers the secret, when every page threatens to bring down doom on the head of the miserable Mark. Will he confess? Will he drown himself? Will Vincent denounce him? Will Caffyn inform on him? Will his wife abandon him?—we ask eagerly as we read and cannot cease reading till the puzzle is solved in a series of exciting situations."

THE PARIAH.

From THE SATURDAY REVIEW.—"In 'The Pariah' we are more than ever struck by the sharp intuitive perception and the satirical balancing of judgment which makes the author's writings such extremely entertaining reading. There is not a dull page—we might say, not a dull sentence—in it. . . . The girls are delightfully drawn, especially the bewitching Margot and the childish Lettice. Nothing that polish and finish, cleverness, humour, wit, and sarcasm can give is left out."

VICE VERSÂ;
OR, A LESSON TO FATHERS.

From THE SATURDAY REVIEW.—"If ever there was a book made up from beginning to end of laughter, and yet not a comic book, or a 'merry' book, or a book of jokes, or a book of pictures, or a jest book, or a tomfool book, but a perfectly sober and serious book, in the reading of which a sober man may laugh without shame from beginning to end, it is the book called 'Vice Versâ; or, a Lesson to Fathers.' . . . ¡We close the book, recommending it very earnestly to all fathers in the first instance, and their sons, nephews, uncles, and male cousins next."

A FALLEN IDOL.

From THE TIMES.—"Mr. Anstey's new story will delight the multitudinous public that laughed over 'Vice Versâ.' . . . The boy who brings the accursed image to Champion's house, Mr. Bales, the artist's factotum, and above all Mr Yarker, the ex-butler who has turned policeman, are figures whom it is as pleasant to meet as it is impossible to forget."